Donald MacKenzie and The Murder Room

››› This title is part of The Murder Room, our series dedicated to making available out-of-print or hard-to-find titles by classic crime writers.

Crime fiction has always held up a mirror to society. The Victorians were fascinated by sensational murder and the emerging science of detection; now we are obsessed with the forensic detail of violent death. And no other genre has so captivated and enthralled readers.

Vast troves of classic crime writing have for a long time been unavailable to all but the most dedicated frequenters of second-hand bookshops. The advent of digital publishing means that we are now able to bring you the backlists of a huge range of titles by classic and contemporary crime writers, some of which have been out of print for decades.

From the genteel amateur private eyes of the Golden Age and the femmes fatales of pulp fiction, to the morally ambiguous hard-boiled detectives of mid twentieth-century America and their descendants who walk our twenty-first century streets, The Murder Room has it all. **›››**

The Murder Room
Where Criminal Minds Meet

themurderroom.com

Donald MacKenzie 1908–1994

Donald MacKenzie was born in Ontario, Canada, and educated in England, Canada and Switzerland. For twenty-five years MacKenzie lived by crime in many countries. 'I went to jail,' he wrote, 'if not with depressing regularity, too often for my liking.' His last sentences were five years in the United States and three years in England, running consecutively. He began writing and selling stories when in American jail. 'I try to do exactly as I like as often as possible and I don't think I'm either psychopathic, a wayward boy, a problem of our time, a charming rogue. Or ever was.'

He had a wife, Estrela, and a daughter, and they divided their time between England, Portugal, Spain and Austria.

Salute from a Dead Man

Donald MacKenzie

An Orion book

Copyright © The Estate of Donald MacKenzie 1966

The right of Donald MacKenzie to be identified as the author of this work has
been asserted in accordance with the Copyright, Designs and Patents Act 1988.

This edition published by
The Orion Publishing Group Ltd
Orion House
5 Upper St Martin's Lane
London WC2H 9EA

An Hachette UK company
A CIP catalogue record for this book is available from the British Library

ISBN 978 1 4719 0491 2

www.orionbooks.co.uk

This novel is dedicated to my friend ADRIAN VAN HALL with the hope that it achieves the standards of story-telling that we both respect.

An extract from the *International Record of Medicine*, April 1956.

". . . This kind of fortuitous observation, or serendipity, occurred in 1943 and, in my opinion, touched off much of the new enquiry into drug effects on the brain. Hoffmann, working in the Sandoz laboratories in Basle, Switzerland, sucked up something in his mouth from a pipette. He had been working with ergot extracts and was making esters of one of its components, lysergic acid. In less than an hour he was muddled, confused and hallucinated. Frightened, he left the laboratory and got on his bicycle. He pedalled what seemed like five thousand miles to his home, which was in reality a short distance away, but he had lost time and space perception. He called his doctor, who managed to get him to gulp down all the milk in the house but his psychotic state persisted until he fell into a fitful sleep that night. Four days later he returned to his laboratory, looked over his notebooks, and decided that he had swallowed the dextro-rotatory diethylamide of lysergic acid. Gingerly he measured out a very minute amount of the material and took another swallow. The psychosis returned, this time worse. He pedalled ten thousand miles home and again drank all the milk in sight to no avail. Thus LSD-25 was born. Here was an experimental way of producing a psychosis that had very much the look and feel of schizophrenia. It takes about one seven-hundred-millionth of a healthy young man's weight of this material to produce a model psychosis lasting five to ten hours."

Ritchie Duncan

THE front of the jail was like the rest of it, old and dirty. Duncan gave his name to the warder on gate duty and stepped through the postern to freedom. A stretch of tarmac the size of a football field faced him. The Governor's house was on the left, on the right that of the Senior Medical Officer. Both dwellings formed an integral part of the prison. This seemed constructed to repel an assault rather than to prevent inmates from escaping. Built in the days of convict-quarried granite, its massive walls and turrets were capable of resisting a tank-battering.

Duncan drew a deep breath. This was the moment that never failed. The first wonderful minutes when your senses played tricks. The light was somehow clearer than ever before, the girls prettier, the future brighter. He slung the camel hair coat round his shoulders, wearing it over his grey flannel suit like a cape. He started across the stretch of tarmac. The suitcase he carried contained everything he owned. A few photographs, a pair of slacks, loafers and a sweater—as many shirts as had withstood the haphazard laundering of forgotten girl friends.

He was halfway to the bus-stop when he heard his name called. A blue E-type Jaguar was parked twenty yards away. A blonde looking about sixteen was behind the wheel, busy with her nails. The man sitting beside her signalled frantically to catch Duncan's attention, then opened his door and came over on the trot. He had a full, smiling mouth and went to a good tailor. A grey streak divided a head of springy black hair.

"Where you running to—don't you talk to your old mates any more?"

It was a second or two before Duncan recognized a one-time cell-partner. Jail uniform made dandies out of bums, turned elegant men into tramps. He remembered Chalice as a hard-core villain—one of a band of extroverts who charged into banks wearing stocking masks and swinging pickaxe shafts. Chalice had befriended him from the first day. They had worked side by side, darning mail-bags filthy with the dust and spittle of countless railroad stations, talking from the corners of their mouths. He had heard Chalice's story one hundred and eleven times. A bad identification, a lazy judge and jury, had combined to put him away for a caper of which he knew nothing. Two months after his conviction, Chalice had been hauled into court on a further charge of bank-robbery. Fate had so disposed events that a finding of guilty on the first charge made it impossible for him to have been on the scene of the second.

Duncan stuck his hand out. "What's the matter, can't you keep away from the place?"

Chalice rubbed the grey streak of hair. "I came up to get old Bumpeye. All that charley on the gate will say is 'He ain't due for release!' You got any idea what happened to him, Ritchie?"

Duncan nodded. "He hit the basket, Harry—claimed the Governor was a pimp in Alexandria during the war. Trouble was he picked on the Governor to say it to. That cost him a week's remission and three days bread-and-water."

Chalice whistled, looking back over his shoulder. "Hear that, Kathy? Bumpeye's done his nut in there!"

The blonde continued to buff her nails. Chalice excused himself ceremoniously to Duncan. He walked to the parked car looking like a leopard about to leap.

"What's the matter?" he demanded pugnaciously. "Don't you hear me when I speak or something?"

The girl focussed cool blue eyes on him. "With the noise *you* make! That's a stupid question. I'm hungry. I want to go home and have some breakfast."

Chalice turned away with a sound of disgust. "Why don't you come and have breakfast with us?" he asked Duncan. "She thinks she's a right giggle but she's not human before ten. Don't pay no attention to her."

The girl switched on the motor. A powerful rumble sounded in the twin exhaust. Duncan hefted his suitcase.

"I'll take a rain-check on it, Harry. Thanks all the same."

Chalice grabbed his arm, leading him a discreet distance from the car. His eyes were solicitous.

"Do you need a few quid, Canada? It's there if you want it."

"I'm loaded," lied Duncan. "I'll see you around, Harry."

The concern left Chalice's face. "You know where to find me—The Red Lion, Stacey Street. Leave a message with the Irishman. And be lucky, do you hear?"

Chalice took his place beside the girl, letting his right arm trail through the open window. He lifted it as the car drove off.

Duncan carried his bag over, glad that the bus-stop was deserted. It was two years since he had been alone. In an English jail it was no longer possible. The Prison Commissioners called the scheme "Associated labour and recreation." The mechanics were that you worked together, walked together, went to the latrine together. To ensure that you understood the benefits of comradeship, you slept three in a cell designed ninety years before for one.

He stopped the northbound bus and mounted to the top deck. He lit his first cigarette at liberty. Jail would have been the place to kick the habit. Kick hell, he added mentally. People had been after him all his life—wagging their fingers, telling him to kick some habit or other. As a direct consequence he'd run every good thing into the ground. He paid for his ticket and opened Martin Pole's letter. It was written on the lawyer's stationery and was characteristically brief.

Dear Ritchie:

    I'd be glad if you would call here at ten a.m. on the morning of your release.

All the best, yours
Martin.

It was the first and last letter Duncan had received in prison. Not that this mattered. Letters inside were a form of tyranny. He'd seen men drive themselves crazy as they searched trite phrases for hidden meanings, demanding explanations for the inexplicable. He put the envelope in an inside pocket and turned his wrist. Half-past-eight. He'd find a decent cup of coffee and a barber. You had to be presentable for Martin. He was more than just a lawyer—he was an old lady with a mirror on the street and an intense interest in other people's affairs—especially those of the Duncan family. Though come to think of it, why not. Anyone who controlled the English end of a million-dollar trust fund was likely to be interested in the beneficiaries.

It was precisely ten when he took the express elevator to the top floor. Pole and Redding's offices were in a modern block overlooking the Thames. A corner of the Reception room had been transformed into an indoor garden. Begonias grew among desert plants. A lifesize statue gazed benignly through the ceiling-to-floor windows. A girl met his glance · of enquiry, smiling.

"Good morning, sir. May I help you?"

She said it with grace and the obvious knowledge that she was pretty.

Duncan put his suitcase down. "I'm Ritchie Duncan. I have an appointment with Mr. Pole."

Her smile made him feel both wanted and important. "Of course, Mr. Duncan. Will you please come this way."

He followed her into a room with pale green walls. There were no briefs or law-books—just Swedish furniture and a Hermes diary. The man who greeted Duncan looked more like a successful actor than a lawyer. His dark suit was fashionably cut. He wore boned black shoes and a knitted silk tie. His trim chestnut-coloured hair was parted on the right side. Except for the final vowel sound, his Canadian accent was almost lost.

"Hello, Ritchie. It's good to see you about!"

They sat in front of immense windows opening on a flat roof. Outside was a sheltered squash-court. A couple of men in shorts were banging a ball about vigorously. Duncan stretched his legs as far as they would go.

" 'Healthy mind in a healthy body.' That's quite a layout you've got here, Martin."

Pole would take his time coming to the point. Meanwhile you had to say something. The lawyer brushed the ends of his eyebrows with a forefinger.

"At least there's no excuse for putting on weight. How was it this time, Ritchie—or would you rather not talk about it?"

Duncan brought the tips of his shoes together and considered them. "This time" was typical.

"Why *should* I mind talking about it? The food was lousy —the company questionable. And it's a drag not being able to lock your own door. What else did you want to know, Martin?"

Far below on the river, two dots in single sculls fought their way upstream, rolling in the wash from a string of barges. Over on the south bank, tugs were manœuvring tankers into their moorings. Pole watched it all with approval—as if he had a hand in the scheme.

"I suppose the authorities argue that they didn't ask you to go there," he observed mildly enough.

Duncan corrected him. "Not the authorities. That's Martin Pole speaking, deep in his tiny shrivelled heart. I've got a busy day ahead, Martin. What did you bring me here for?"

Pole laughed and hung his head, his hands pushed deep in his trouser pockets. It was a strong portrayal of the legal mind being composed to firm kindness.

"I've had lots of correspondence with Flora while you were in jail, Ritchie. Naturally, she's been deeply concerned by your last escapade. You can imagine what the newspapers did with it at home. The news broke five days before Cam arrived in England. It followed him up to Oxford. That's a pretty damned unpleasant thing to live down in your first term."

Duncan frowned. The last time he had seen Flora's son, the kid had a bow and arrow and no front teeth.

"I'm sorry about that," he said shortly. "Flora ought to know that I didn't pick the time or the place."

Pole waved magnanimously. "That's obvious. I'll put it on the line, Ritchie. I happen to think the old man should never have cut you out of the trust. And on that score the family votes three to two against you. You know as well as I do which two they are. They've shown their feelings in a practical way in the past. There's little more they can do. The terms of the trust deed are foolproof."

They were and no was likely to let him forget it. Duncan answered bluntly. "Come off it, Martin. My sister and Hector have drawn fifteen thousand dollars a year each for the last ten years, without making any impression on the capital. During those years I've had exactly eighteen hundred dollars from Flora. Hector paid for my defence on one occasion—we'll call that two thousand bucks. That makes three eight in all. What the hell are they looking for—a tax rebate?"

Pole's expression hardened. "Now wait a minute—you haven't been in Canada in eight years. Things have changed. It's *what* you are today not who that counts. But the name Duncan is still respected in Toronto—everyone in the family would like to keep it that way. Even the kids are old enough to have made up their minds about you, Ritchie—and they have. You're out—a dead member."

Duncan answered without rancour. "I was never in. The kids don't know me—only what they've been told about me. You're the one who mentioned money, Martin. I never asked anyone for a nickel. I've tried to lead my own life without involving others. I'm deeply sorry if it's affected Flora's children. I'd like her to know that. The hell with the others."

"But it's such a goddamned waste," Pole burst out. "You've got a good mind and you've done absolutely nothing with it. Look at the record. Ski-instructor; night-club photographer; space salesman. I guess the best one could say was that these were at least honest. Then you start breaking into people's houses and stealing their jewellery. *Stealing*, Ritchie! Even the idea ought to bother you. You're not a

8

burglar—you're not even good at it. How many convictions have you had in five years—three, is it? What's going to happen to you finally—or don't you care?"

Duncan watched the squash players but remembered the old con man in Paris. Drunk, Melaney had talked for an hour about a more leisurely age of rascality—of state-rooms on ocean liners—of marks hooked by the larceny in their own hearts. Suddenly he'd drawn himself up on the bar-stool, clutching the edge of the counter.

"Most thieves," he'd said in a loud clear voice, "die in the poorhouse or the pisshole. Right off the top of my head, I'd say my exit will combine both places."

Duncan lowered his chair on its front legs. "I care enough to be doing something about it. Exactly what is my affair—nobody else's."

Pole sat down again, his voice and manner coaxing. "Listen, Ritchie—the family's empowered me to act as their agent. They're offering you twenty thousand dollars payable in Australia. What they ask in return is that you renounce the name Duncan legally. I've prepared the necessary documents."

Duncan looked back impassively. Pole's smile weakened. "You just bought yourself a sack of fish-hooks," said Duncan. "I've been Ritchie Duncan for thirty-six years. It'll take more than a paddle-arsed lawyer and money to make me change. Tell the family that with my compliments."

Pole did his best with a show of patience. "You haven't let me finish. There's a job waiting for you in Queensland. Someone we know well in this office needs a man to train as manager. When you talk about sheep-stations these days, you don't mean shacks where guys in their underwear brew tea in billycans. This is a modern business run on scientific lines. Two hundred thousand acres—a ranch-house with plumbing. Horses, gum-trees, prospects. Gabriel flies up there from Sydney twice a year. If he takes a liking to you, there's no telling where it might end."

Duncan gathered himself together. "It ends right here, Martin, old boy. I've *got* a job. The sort of job Hector would approve of for me—hard work for little money. Eight pounds a week basic pay and what I make in tips as barman. If you ever show your nose in the joint I'll slip you a mickey."

Pole shrugged an elegant acceptance of defeat. "I guess you know what you're doing, Ritchie. But there's an obverse side to the coin. The next time you drag the family name into the gutter-press we're going to hit you hard. And there are ways."

Duncan swung round, his eyes savage. "Don't ever threaten me, Martin. And when you feel like putting your foot in your mouth again, remember your name's Pole. *I'm* the Duncan." He pulled the doorhandle behind him.

The receptionist brightened her smile for him. "Shall I call a cab for you, Mr. Duncan? I can have one at the door by the time you get downstairs."

He kept the bitterness out of his voice and kidded. "Don't ever let it get beyond this office but there's one Duncan who walks."

He picked up his bag and headed for the fast ride down. 120 Tierney Street was a tall thin building wedged between a bank and garage. The framework of the front door was studded with bell-pushes. As far as Duncan could see, the tenants were identified by occupation. He read the right-hand sequence.

PINCUS PLOTKIN, MANUFACTURER'S AGENT THE PACERS—
THE DANCING ACT WITH A DIFFERENCE MADAME SONYA—
CLAIRVOYANCE AND COMMUNICATION

Beneath the bottom bell was a plate that read RESIDENT CARETAKER. He leaned his thumb on it. Some time passed before the door was opened by a small man wearing a flat cloth cap and carpet slippers. Satin evening braces in a state of extreme decay supported trousers several sizes too large for him. He peered out as if memorizing every detail of Duncan's appearance.

"Wotcher want?" he asked suspiciously.

Duncan tendered the slip of paper. "I understand you've a room for me. I was told to give you this."

The caretaker brought the paper close to his nose and nodded. "I gotcher. Foller me."

He led the way into a dreary hall paved with linoleum. A notice hung from the coat rack.

TIERNEY SERVICE FLATLETS
HOT & COLD. TELEPHONE
PROFESSIONAL PEOPLE WELCOME
RENTS STRICTLY MONTHLY IN ADVANCE

The caretaker shuffled like a crab to the bottom of the stairs and grunted his way up to the second storey. Here he unlocked a door. The back room had one large window and simple furniture. A divan bed, a couple of chairs and small table, a clothes-closet made of hardboard. An unframed mirror hung over the wash-basin. The caretaker perched on the edge of the bed, wheezing.

"You pay as you go—gas, telephone, the lot. It's all meters, see. There's no washing clothes in your room—no all-night visitors—no 'ollering and 'ooting after midnight." He filled his lungs with air and finished on a note of deep pessimism. "It's a waste of time but it's what I'm supposed to tell yer."

Duncan tried the faucets. The water ran rusty, cleared and then bubbled with heat. He draped his overcoat on a hanger in the closet.

"I'll try to remember. Thanks."

The caretaker showed no signs of going but sat, slippered feet dangling. He spoke in a hoarse confidential whisper.

"'Ow long were you in for?"

Duncan let the shirts fall back in his suitcase. "What did you say?"

The divan creaked as the old man shifted. His rheumy eyes were curious but without malice.

"'Ow long did you do? You don't 'ave to worry about me —we've 'ad dozens of 'em 'ere. The guvnor's partial to a bit of philanthropy—especially when 'e's sure of 'is rent."

Duncan resumed his unpacking. His skin would have to get a lot tougher before he'd finished with rehabilitation.

"Three years. And if it's all right with you I'd like to forget about it."

The caretaker showed bare gums. " 'Joe' they call me. If you're a foreigner, you'll 'ave to sign the Aliens Book."

Duncan tugged the curtains aside. The weed-grown yard below was hideous with legless chairs, a gutted sofa, broken packing-cases. He pulled the top sash down, letting in fresh air.

"Don't let it worry you. Was there anything else you wanted?"

The caretaker took the hint but stopped at the door. He made his claim to acceptance in a stage-whisper.

"I been inside meself only 'e don't know it—'undreds of times! Drunk and disorderly. 'The terror of Chapel St.!' they used to call me. Me room's at the bottom of the stairs. If you need me 'oller. If you don't get no answer I'll be 'avin a nap in the warm. In the boilerouse, see. Tata!"

Duncan cocked his thumb. The caretaker winked and shut the door quietly. Duncan emptied his pockets and hung the grey flannel suit with his overcoat. He donned slacks and sweater and reread the sheet of instructions.

Proceed to 120 Tierney Street, Putney, where a room has been taken for you. Report as soon as possible (but NOT before 11.30 a.m.) to Mr. Dave Henschel at the Cintra Bar, 1169 Putney High Street.

It was eleven-twenty. He balled the piece of paper and threw it at the trash-basket. He found the Cintra at the summit of the long slope. The entrance was at the end of an arcade, next to a dental surgery. He pushed the glass doors. The long room smelled of last night's liquor. The bar occupied half one wall. Dusty Andalusian hats, beribboned guitars and castanets hung on the others. A shirtsleeved man in his forties was leaning on the bar. He had a flat nose, padded checkbones and crouching shoulders. His cigar looked as if it had served as breakfast.

Duncan nodded at him pleasantly. "Mr. Henschel? I'm

Ritchie Duncan. The After-Care Association said you'd be expecting me."

"Half-an-hour ago," Henschel said morosely. He switched the cigar to the other side of his mouth. "The job's what you make of it. I've got a good eye and I can count. We don't serve whores or niggers—anyone else's money is good. And we mind our own business. OK?"

"OK," said Duncan and approached the bar.

"Good," answered Henschel. "You start tonight at six. I supply jackets and aprons. There's just one thing. You'll be working with a monkey who knows you've been inside. It's a pity but it couldn't be helped. He was hanging around when the man from the A.C.A. called. What he didn't hear he invented for himself. I never knew it but it turns out he once lost a bird to a burglar. He's never forgotten it. I don't want any trouble between you. I've already told him."

Duncan took the beer Henschel slid along the bar. It was icecold and heady—the first in two years.

"It takes two to make that kind of trouble."

Henschel gave the prospect moody consideration. "You might say I'm the punch-up expert round here. We get all kinds. Business people, some of the kids from Reilly's gym, the odd villain. We don't ask customers for good-conduct certificates—just to behave themselves. I like a man to be able to bring his wife in here or a bird without someone having a go at them. And I don't encourage the law. First thing you know it gets to be a habit and they don't pay for drinks. I'm taking a chance on you for old times' sake. I had a good year in Canada. No big purses but a good year. That's the main thing to remember, Duncan—no law in here not on no pretext."

Duncan downed his beer. September sun touched the top of the bar, exposing the cigarette burns, the ringed reminders of countless glasses. A trapped fly buzzed in the belly of the guitar hanging on the wall. It was a shabby room in the golden light—oppressive with a sense of dreams exploded even as they were formulated. A second rate bar for second rate people. He had an urge to put his broken-

13

nosed benefactor straight on a couple of matters. He waited till Henschel turned from his bottles.

"I get the message. You've given your reason for hiring me—now I'll give you mine for taking the job. It's the end of a period in my life, no more, no less. Someone reminded me this morning that I wasn't even a good thief. He argued that three convictions in five years didn't add up to the essence of intelligence. He was right but he forgot one thing —I earned an honest living for twelve years, if you'll excuse the term 'honest'. When I move on, I don't know where I'm going. But you can bet your nose on one thing—it won't be a place where they give me a number to match my name."

Henschel's fingers wandered to his scalp. His small eyes were sunk against the sunshine. "What's that mean—that you're here for the weekend?"

Duncan shook his head. "My room costs me fifteen quid a month. You're supposed to give me two meals a day. I can save on that. I *mean* to save. Just as soon as I've gotten a couple of hundred quid together, I'm off—on deep water, Mr. Henschel. That's the way it is."

Henschel opened the door behind the bar and spoke a few words to the cleaning woman. The dead cigar bobbed in his face.

"Beginner barmen aren't hard to get. Now I been all over —the biggest fight cities in the world. Where you going to head for?"

Duncan smiled. "I'd be disappointed if I knew that 'Chance is powerful everywhere. Let your hook be always hanging ready' as the guy said."

Henschel scratched his armpit thoughtfully. "*Who* said— Churchill?"

"Ovid," answered Duncan. "All I do know is that it won't be Australia."

Henschel's reveries were over. "You be here at six. And while I think about it—the only person who calls me 'Mr. Henschel' is the Income Tax Inspector. Otherwise I'm Dave."

The elderly woman carried a pail of water into the bar.

She went down on her knees. Duncan lifted the stools on the tables for her.

"Six on the dot," he said. "With my hair brushed and a big smiling face. And thanks."

Hugh Morgan

HE lifted his head slowly, his thin face composed to caution. His hands had started to shake. The heavy desk hid the lower half of his body from the girl standing across the room. He leaned forward, secretly nudging the drawer with his knee. He fumbled the key round in the lock, looking over the girl's shoulder at the door beyond. His own stained mac was there on the hook, the brown coat. But her handbag was missing. He stalled for time as she continued to watch him—a tall girl in her late twenties, willowy and underweight.

She dabbed vaguely at reddish swinging hair, her sherry-coloured eyes troubled. The fine skin on her forehead was etched with frown-lines. She came towards him, moving as though her legs were tied at the knees. She wore pale lipstick on a wide mouth. Her clothes could have been bought at any medium-budget store. She stopped in front of the desk, producing the handbag from behind her back with what was almost a theatrical gesture. She tipped out its contents. Keys and coins rang on the desk. A wallet fell opened on a snapshot of Morgan enclosed in a cellophane window. The phial of seltzer tablets rolled into his lap. He placed it back on the blotter, watching her hands. They too were shaking. The small topaz on her engagement finger was only slightly darker than her eyes. She unscrewed the top of the phial and shook out a couple of tablets. The cotton wad he had used to plug the tube gave her trouble. She pried it loose with a hairgrip. A foil-wrapped roll of film plopped out. She looked and sounded bewildered.

"Did you put this in my bag, Hugh?"

He shrugged, letting bitterness tinge the brief smile. Discovery had come without drama. There'd been no thunderous summons on the door as day broke with the last incriminating scraps of paper smouldering in the fire-grate. Blue suit and clean white collar--"Gentlemen, I believe you are waiting for me!" No banner headline--"Communist Agent Unmasked!" Just a flatulent bitch with a bellyache. He revived the smile, hiding his hatred. Even in this she hadn't been capable of consistency. For months the bicarbonate tablets had been as indispensable as her lipstick. She never varied their use. One after her morning coffee, the other after her lunch-break. It was some time since he had had the idea of using the phials to smuggle film off the premises. To retrieve whatever he planted on her had always been simple. He remembered the formula with distaste. The long walk home along the river bank, kicking their way through summer grass or wet sandwiched leaves. The hand that would shyly creep into his—the cheek pressed against his sleeve. Banal preliminaries to the farce of hold-ing her naked body against his. Then her coy exit to the bathroom, huddled in his robe. Once the door had closed, he would search her bag, collecting the planted film.

Then she'd stand in the darkened hall and thank him. "Thank you, Hugh, darling!" she said breathlessly.

He lit a cigarette without answering. The pulse in her throat was erratic.

"I've got to know," she said desperately.

The clock showed a quarter-to-five. Another fifteen minutes and the offices would be closed for the night. It was unlikely that they would be disturbed. He touched the roll of film with a tentative finger.

"You know what this is, of course?"

She looked at him but said nothing. He spread his hands.

"What's the use of trying to explain—what sort of chance have I got? You see everything as either black or white."

Her eyes were intensely sad. "Listen to me, Hugh. You're not talking to a stranger. I love you. Doesn't that help?"

He pushed back his chair and walked as far as the window. The sodden lawns outside sloped away to a high brick wall that followed the line of the towpath. November fog hung over the river, obscuring the bank on the far side. A hundred yards away, barbed-wire surrounded a compound. The nerve-centre of Faraday Electronic Research was a sprawl of one-storeyed buildings, built like bank-vaults and windowless. A cement shaft dominated the skyline, looking like a control tower on an airfield. This was Block A—Security—housing the closed television circuits, the Dobermans and their handlers—Major Sangster and his guard.

He turned away, speaking to her with the awkwardness he knew she expected.

"Suppose I told you I was a thief, Linda?"

She shut her eyes as he came near her, shivering when his mouth touched her neck. The violence of her sudden movement dislodged his hands.

"I'll love you till the world's upside down—isn't that answer enough?"

He retreated to the desk and sat down, chin up, hands resting lightly on the blotter. His voice was husky.

"Don't judge me too quickly, Linda. That film represents the difference between what I am and what I hope to be. Think of that."

The strain showed in the working of her mouth. "I don't judge you, Hugh. But it's like loving a sphinx. Sometimes I feel that deep down you resent me—that sharing your life is something completely intolerable to you."

He took her hand in his. The inside of her left wrist was crisscrossed with scars. He stroked her flesh gently.

"You know that's not true, Linda. Your father commanded a regiment. I never knew mine. I never even knew who he was. I'm a polytechnic graduate with the wrong sort of accent—living in a council flat. Do you think these things are easy to forget?"

Colour flared in her pale face. "You're all I have in the world."

His tongue touched his lips. "But that's not enough. I

have to have something to offer you. This film is worth ten thousand pounds to a French electronics firm. I'm not ashamed of what I've done, darling. I wouldn't be ashamed of anything that made our marriage something more than just a dream."

Her nails dug deep into his palm. "I'd defend you if you'd committed murder, Hugh. Why don't you trust me?"

He answered with quick glibness. "I'm not sure that I trusted myself let alone you. I hid the film in your bag because you have an A pass and I don't. You're safe from a search. If I'd told you, your very manner could have given you away. Surely you see that?"

It was sketchy and weak with too many loopholes. She would know that he had no access to classified information —that this was kept in the strong-room, protected by a complicated security system. He was a thirty-four-year-old records clerk not a safebreaker. Sooner or later she would remind herself of that.

She moved unexpectedly, catching him by the shoulders and pulling him to her. She pressed her mouth tightly on his and then let him go.

"I don't want to hear anything more, Hugh. I'm a much better actress than you imagine. I'm going to take the film out and bring it wherever you like. But you must promise me one thing."

Her starry-eyed enthusiasm moved him to contempt. "Anything, Linda. You know that."

She put on her coat and cut all the lights save that on his desk. She looked younger, more sure of herself.

"This must be the last time. You must never do anything like this again. I'd sooner scrub floors than see you in danger. I can't even bear to think about it."

"We don't *need* another time," he said soberly. The Fate Sisters had been good to him.

She smiled, brightly and nervously. "Where do you want me to meet you?"

"The *Cintra*," he said. "At nine. And remember, I love you."

He stood at the window behind curtains that smelled of stale smoke. The deeper grey of twilight had swallowed the fog. As he looked, the floodlights came on in the compound —the walls and the security tower blazed. A few cars were still parked in front of the Administration wing. He watched the company secretary reverse his Ford and drive off. The first group from Planning was leaving. He eyed them sourly —the Briefcase Brigade— their school ties advertising their background. Idiots conditioned to the continuance of social injustice. The women were worse, using their bodies as squalid bait to hook class-conscious fools and breed still more enemies of progress.

They straggled out, Linda a head taller than most and walking alone. Her face was hidden in the upturned collar, the bag clutched tightly under her right arm. He lit another cigarette, glancing at the tower. Sangster was up there, overseeing the exodus, sniffing out defection. She still had another twenty yards to go. Suddenly she seemed to slow. He dragged the salt burn of tobacco deep into his lungs. A split-second doubt invaded his confidence. *I'm a better actress than you think, Hugh.* And what if it were true? He pictured her handing the film to Sangster, a faint smile on her face. *"No he's still in the office. He reacted exactly the way you said he would."*

His thoughts jumped like a tree squirrel. His fingerprints would be on the foil that wrapped the film. He'd say that the only time he touched it was when she handed the film to him. He sucked in his breath as she came to the junction of paths. She switched her bag to the other arm and turned right towards the gates. He stayed at his post till he saw her on the street outside. She was walking alone.

He unlocked the drawer in his desk and pulled out the small cloth bag. The skeleton keys had been made from the impressions that he had provided. The organization had drilled him in the expertise, culled from God knows what strange source. It had been easier to use than he had imagined. Once a week and for ten minutes, the company secretary's keys hung in a lock in the strong-room door. He had leant against it casually, talking to a girl busy with correspondence. His fingers behind his back had pressed the keys into scraped cuttlefish bone. The impressions had been perfect. Now the keys must be jettisoned.

He reduced the bulk of the Mark V Leica by unscrewing the lens. He stuffed keys and camera inside his shirt and buttoned his mac over them. It was two minutes to five He shut his office door and walked across the deserted Reference Room. Cowled lamps burnt at the tables, the soft light silhouetting the carved balustrade overhead. The library was lodged in what had been a musicians gallery – eighty thousand books and pamphlets covering the history of electronics. He left the lights as they were. One of the guards would turn them off later. He hurried into the main hall. Voices came from the Administration Wing. A man was sitting on a chair just inside the doors leading to the front steps. Two Dobermans rose stiff-legged as Morgan approached. The guard hauled on the leash, hushing the warning rumble in the dogs' throats. He wore bottlegreen battledress and a beret with a badge. He looked over his shoulder at the clock.

"You're running it a bit fine. You don't expect these buggers to be able to tell the time, do you?"

Morgan stepped by gingerly. The entire pack of guard dogs had broken away a few Sundays before. Rumour had it that a gardener had been savaged and taken to hospital. He came to a halt at the bottom of the steps.

"How many of these brutes are running around loose?"

The man shrugged, jerking his thumb at the Administration Wing.

"None. You're safe enough as long as the brains are here."

He shut the front doors as the clock struck the half hour. Morgan picked his way along a ribbon of path, paler than the edging grass. Wet fog drifted into the lights crisscrossing the grounds. He left the path and squelched across soaked turf to crouch at the bottom of a box-hedge. An iron inspection-plate was sunk in the ground. He found the fingerholds and lifted the airtight cover from its bed. He held his breath as sewage gas rose in his face. Lips compressed, he leaned into the hole and smashed the camera against the brickwork. Metal clattered dully below. He dropped the lens after the shattered case and replaced the inspection plate. Acid had been used to etch off the serial numbers from the Leica. He shoved the skeleton keys deep into soft earth and wiped the mud from his fingers.

He started walking towards the Security Tower. Heavy doors swung inwards as his passage broke the photo-electric beam. The room was D-shaped with an immense curved window. Under this were half-a-dozen television screens. Concealed cameras controlled the boundary walls, reproducing a vista of wet trees and shadows. A pair of guards lolled on chairs. Both wore the battledress and beret uniform. One swung round towards Morgan. His look was neither suspicious nor welcoming. He held out a hand, continuing the conversation with his companion.

Morgan produced his pass. "I'd like to see Major Sangster."

The guard manipulated the pass as a gambler does a coin. "It's gone five. You're supposed to be off the premises."

A dog yelped from the basement. The stink of kennels mingled with the smell of the guard's cheroot. Morgan kept his voice civil.

"Perhaps Major Sangster will decide that."

The guard looked as if he found the suggestion superfluous. He handed a pad to Morgan. A cheap pen was wired to the binding.

"Fill the form in!"

Morgan read the printed lines. Name: Pass number: Nature of business:

"It's a personal matter," he said finally.

The guard demonstrated a new way of rolling his eyes for the amusement of his companion.

"It usually is. But you still fill in the form."

Morgan scribbled a few words. The guard flicked a button and spoke into the inter-com. The casualness of his pose

was at variance with his respectful tone. He rose to his feet.
"All right—this way."

Carpeted stairs curled to the upper floor. A door opened
as Morgan reached it. Sangster wore a checked jacket,
cavalry-twill trousers and tasselled shoes. His regimental
tie was tightly knotted. He had a bald brown head, fleshy
nose and womanish mouth. He welcomed Morgan with an
odd sort of throwing gesture. The tower room had the same
sweep of window as below but bookshelves replaced the
television screens. There were some Gauguin prints on the
walls three telephones on a gatelegged table—two of them
coloured. Sangster indicated a seat.

"Sit down, Mr. Morgan. What can we do for you?" He had
the false bonhomie of a liquor-store proprietor. He smiled
mechanically, reaching into a filing-cabinet. He pulled out a
folder and glanced inside as if what he saw was of no
importance to either of them.

Morgan's amusement was interior. He didn't have to read
the file to know approximately what it said.

Hugh Morgan, 34. Bachelor. No known political affilia-
tions. Member of Putney Chess Club. The Friends of
Bach Society. Lives within his salary. Normal sex interests. B pass. Approved for limited access.

He affected a degree of embarrassment. "I just hope I won't
be wasting your time. It's an odd situation. I work with a
Miss Swann. I suppose that the simple thing to say is that
I'm worried about her. It goes a little deeper than that."

The checked arm collected a second file. Sangster toyed
with his mound of nose as he read. He put the folder back
without comment.

"Yes?"

Morgan brushed his hand through the cloud of cigarette-
smoke. "We see quite a lot of one another outside office
hours. You know how these things can start. You're thrown
together, day in, day out. She's a highly nervous girl, under
considerable strain at the moment. If it shows in her work,

22

it must reflect on me. Which would be fair in one way. I'm partly responsible."

Sangster made the same odd flicking gesture. "Are you able to talk in anything simpler than riddles?"

Morgan hesitated. "It's a delicate matter."

Sangster leaned forward, emphasizing his point. "When you joined us, you made a declaration under the Official Secrets Act. It isn't a gag for fools but a pledge of undivided loyalty to your employers. In this instance, that means me. What is the matter between you and Miss Swann?"

Morgan teased him along. "Nothing except emotional instability. I've said we see a great deal of one another. The relationship seems to matter more to her than it does to me. She expects marriage, Major Sangster. For someone like me that's impossible."

Sangster's small eyes considered Morgan shrewdly. "What's wrong with the idea?"

Morgan lifted his shoulders hopelessly. "I should have thought that was obvious, Major Sangster. We don't really have anything in common. I've enough sense to realize that this sort of marriage is doomed to failure. She refuses to accept this. It's an extremely difficult position. Miss Swann has been through something like this before. It affected her in a drastic fashion. She was under psychiatric treatment for a very long time. I wouldn't want it to happen again."

Sangster pulled a file again. He sat with it on his knees for a while reading. Morgan stared through the window. A guard walked a brace of Dobermans over the wet grass. One of the animals sniffed the ground where the keys had been buried then lifted its leg. Sangster raised his head.

"Miss Swann's record is excellent. Not a black mark against her in the five years she's worked here. I'm concerned with facts not psychiatric mumbo-jumbo."

Morgan's voice was anxious. "Files only tell you so much about a man. I wouldn't be working here if money was all that mattered to me. I have a sense of belonging at Faraday's—a feeling of being part of the future. I believe that hard work will achieve recognition anywhere in the long run. Scandal would kill any chance of promotion. That's really why I came to see you tonight. To give you the facts."

Sangster clasped his hands behind his neck, the shadow of his nose a great wen on the wall.

"I understand you're a chess-player. How good are you?"

Morgan's smile was rueful. "I belong to a club with twenty-three members. I've never managed to get beyond the first round of our annual tournament."

Sangster cut in impatiently. "But you're supposed to have a disciplined mind. I'm not running a Lonely Hearts Bureau. The advice comes gratis. A disciplined mind has no room for emotional extravagance. You do a very good job here, Morgan. I'm going to arrange for Miss Swann to be transferred to another department. This will give you an excuse to let the association cool off a little. Then kill it. More than that I can't suggest. Good night."

The guard waiting at the foot of the stairs slung a waterproof cape round his shoulders, his face sour.

"Where's it supposed to be buried this time?"

"Where's *what* supposed to be buried?" replied Morgan.

The guard affected astonishment. "The bomb, mate. That old bomb ticking away that you bleeders think you hear twice a week." Someone in the tower touched a switch, lighting the stretch to the lodge-gate. Morgan swung in beside the guard. He surrendered his office keys to the gatekeeper and punched the time-clock.

MORGAN, H. out 17 hrs. 18

He turned west into a region of stuccoed houses backing on the Thames and screened from the road by a ramble of trees and shrubbery. Mixed mist and fog billowed through gateways, touching the brickwork with moisture. The air was raw and choking. He walked as he usually did when alone, rapidly and close to the wall. It was inevitable that the organization would criticize him. Justified or not, this was part of the discipline. They spoke about danger as if they invented it and had no praise for its avoidance.

He bought an afternoon paper outside the subway station and used it as a screen while waiting for the phone booths to empty. The first homebound rush of workers was fighting its way through the exits. He watched them with cold appraisal seeing renegades ready to betray their own cause—believers in status symbols rather than brotherhood. He slipped into a free booth and dialled a number. A girl's voice was quick in answer.

"Good evening—Sidney Penner's."

He spoke slowly and distinctly. "Philip Hindin, account number H 216." He heard the call switched, gave the code signal to a familiar voice. "I want five pounds each way the third favourite at White City tonight."

The man read back the bet. "You're Mr. Philip Hindin, H 216. You want five pounds each way the third favourite at White City, ten pounds invested. Thank you, Mr. Hindin, you're on."

Morgan wiped sticky hands. The message would reach its destination in a matter of minutes. How and where no longer interested him. What mattered was that the organization acted promptly. A woman with blue hair and an outraged expression was rapping on the glass with her umbrella. He brushed past and bought a ticket. A tired collector waved him down the stairs. He stood in the crowded westbound train, his eyes photographing his neighbours, assessing those who alighted at the same station. He loitered in the booking-hall, glancing at the clock from time to time like a man uncertain of an appointment. When the last passenger had left, Morgan went out to the street. Drizzle had thinned the fog. Wet sidewalks reflected a vista of neon-lit stores. Late shoppers ducked into supermarkets for the last illusion of fellowship before returning to their bed-sitting rooms.

Morgan crossed the railroad tracks and turned right halfway up Wimbledon Hill. The long street ahead was dreary under the fine rain. Sad squares of privet-hedged gardens fronted the houses. He stopped a hundred yards on. The gate creaked as he pushed it open. He walked up the narrow path to the porch. The street-door had painted-glass panels. A tarnished plate screwed to the wall said:

HAROLD CLEVELAND   MASSAGE AND BONE
MANIPULATION
LICENSED BY THE L.C.C.
CONSULTATIONS BY APPOINTMENT ONLY

The curtains behind the bow windows in the front room were tightly drawn. The only light came from somewhere beyond the hall. Morgan bent down, pushing the mail flap up as far as it would go. There was a strong smell of frying onions but he saw nothing. A strip of felt blocked his vision. He rattled the flap impatiently and waited in a corner of the porch. He was completely hidden from the street. Rain gurgled in the guttering overhead. The six o'clock news boomed from the neighbouring houses. He peered out as someone unfastened the bolts on the side door. He stepped over the pots of hydrangeas, feeling his way past the front windows. A hand reached from the darkness, taking hold of his arm. It guided him down a passage between fence and wall. The kitchen door opened and shut quickly. His guide had the peaked face of a dyspeptic. He hooked his overcoat on a nail, revealing a surgical jacket and trousers badly in need of a bleach. His sleeves were rolled up to the elbows, the muscles of his forearms knotted and exaggerated. He turned down the flame under a frying-pan and led the way through the shabby dining-room into the dim hall. A moth-eaten stag's head grinned at the bottom of the stairs. A selection of caps perched on its antlers. The masseur smiled primly.

"Don't keep him waiting. You know the way."

A button clicked and the hall was in complete darkness. The door at the head of the stairs was ajar, the room stuffy with heat from the gas-fire. There was an old-maid neatness about the place. There were lace mats under the vases. A table was decked with yellow chrysanthemums and dated photographs. Morgan took the chair by the fire. The man sprawling on the divan was a stranger. His stiff decent clothes gave him a peculiarly respectable appearance. Most of his short neck was concealed by a high collar. His greying hair was clipped short above the ears, the longer strands artfully arranged on top. A ragged scar running from forehead to crown showed through the thin locks. His voice was low-pitched yet distinct, like that of a priest in a confessional.

"Are the mountains high in your part of the world?"

"Some are higher than others," Morgan answered.

The stranger sat up straight. "My name's Ashe. What precautions did you take coming here?"

Morgan shed his raincoat. A number of butts floated in the pan of water in front of the fire. The brand name was the same as that on the pack by Ashe's side. The man must have been in the house for some time. Morgan spoke drily.

"I did a course a couple of years ago. By the time they'd finished with me I was able to describe anyone following me down to the colour of his socks. In addition to that, I lost their best man five times."

Ashe ran a finger inside his boot. He had a trick of nodding vigorously as if in encouragement.

"Did you bring the film with you?"

Morgan answered confidently. "No but you'll have it tonight. I take it you know about the girl at Faraday's—the one I work with?"

Ashe removed the cigarette from his mouth, his voice sardonic. "Suppose we put things in proper perspective. You can take it for granted that the only thing I *don't* know about you is why you're here tonight. An emergency call means added risk for everyone concerned. I'm sure you've thought of that."

There was something ominous in the way it was said, Morgan thought. Yet if it hadn't been for him, there'd *be* no film nor any of the others that had gone before.

He broke the news reluctantly. "The emergency call was necessary. I'm afraid she found the film in her bag this afternoon. But she still took it off the premises. She believed what I told her. She thinks I'm selling trade secrets to Faraday's competitors for money to marry her with."

Ashe nodded away, his eyes shut tight. "When and where are you meeting this woman?"

Morgan tried to make his voice reassuring. "At nine o'clock tonight—in a bar at the top of Putney High Street—the Cintra. You can forget about her—there are no problems. She happens to be in love with me. That's more important to her than fear or a sense of moral duty. She'll ask no questions—she won't talk. She'll just do as she's told. I'll vouch for that."

Ashe opened his eyes. They were singularly penetrating. "That sort of optimism ends in disaster. You haven't the right to vouch for anything—not even me. You're in danger. She can destroy your use at any moment. She'll have to go. I want a report on this woman as complete as you can make it. Her home, family, habits and friends." He spoke as a man might do, arranging the despatch of some marauding animal—completely without passion.

Morgan hid his dirty cuffs, one part of his brain wondering whether his laundry would have been delivered. As soon as he trusted his voice he answered.

"You're saying what I've known since the moment she opened her handbag. In fact I've already done something about it. I saw the security people on my way out tonight. They wouldn't exactly be surprised if something happened to her. If she committed suicide, for example. She's tried it once before."

Ashe pocketed his cigarettes. He looked like a farmer readying himself for home, a good market day behind him.

"You talk too much," he said bleakly. "You have too many ideas—all of them of doubtful value. Your stupidity's achieved enough for one day."

Morgan picked up his raincoat. The cheap material was soaked. His hands were shaking with anger. He controlled himself, remembering the beginning of all this ironically. He'd been so patient—so dedicated to make that first contact. The Hands-Off-China movement had met weekly in a hall smelling of chalk off the North End Road. A handful of men and women who sat round rickety tables drinking lemon-tea and discussing action by the people. His own speech had come after a month's waiting and watching, a vehement statement of China's right to the bomb. A stranger had waited for him in the vestibule afterwards. An elderly shabby man with shrewd violet eyes. They'd walked together to the Fulham Road and had drunk bad coffee till the place closed. He'd talked freely, sensing a brain trained to scout likely sympathizers. Three months later he was a party member. A year after that had come the order to apply for the job at Faraday's. Since then he'd read every report of a spy trial that he could lay his hands on. Fuchs, Abel, the Rosenbergs. Every Communist agent who had failed. The lesson was apparent. The Party had its own ways of ensuring loyalty in its unpaid ranks. He had avoided the obvious traps. But he had an uneasy feeling that now he might have sprung one of his own making. He did his best to appear at ease. "What do you want me to do?"

Ashe tucked the bottoms of his trousers into his socks. He strapped on a pair of leggings.

"Get rid of her as soon as you've got the film in your possession. Go to Putney Bridge at ten o'clock—the upstream side. You'll see a black Humber—EPB 47. The driver will take you to Hammersmith Broadway. Give him the film and whatever information you can supply about the girl. Wear the same clothes."

He left the room. Morgan stayed till he heard the motorcycle stutter up the road. Ashe was just another would-be commissar—with the same parade of omnipotence as the rest of the foreign contacts. Morgan groped his way downstairs, unable to find the light switch. The door opened suddenly. The masseur stood there smiling. Morgan stripped to his shorts and stretched out on the rubbing-table. The man's fingers dug skilfully, kneaded Morgan's muscles. His thumbs were almost caressing on Morgan's throat.

"He didn't stay long, did he?" he asked quietly. "I think you must have upset him?"

Morgan rolled sideways. "That's enough." He swung his feet to the ground and wiped his body with a towel.

Sweat pearled the masseur's forehead. His breath stank of the fried onions. He shook his head doubtfully.

"You're jumpy tonight. You should learn to relax."

He wrote out his bill as Morgan dressed. The organization was run with method. Morgan had been supplied with a cover story for every contact he'd made—down to the copy of "West's Common Wildfowl" that gave an alternative reason to his wanderings in parks. The Hands-Off-China movement had long-since been disbanded, its followers believers in a flat world or the like. He had come far since then and in safety. A safety that only Linda's death could ensure. Ashe was right enough about that.

He let himself out to the street, hearing the masseur retreat down the passage, singing in a flat tenor. The drizzle had intensified. A light wind drove it from behind, soaking the backs of his legs. At the bottom of the hill, the queues at the bus-stops huddled under umbrellas. He stood for a while on the end of a line. A cab unloaded a passenger outside the station. He sidestepped through the traffic and poked his head through the window. The driver's face soured as he heard the destination.

"Putney? And what happens afterwards? I could wait all night for a fare to bring me back."

Morgan opened the rear door. "I'll pay fare-and-a-half. If you don't like the arrangement we can always ask a policeman to settle it."

The driver twisted his head round. "One of those, eh? No, mate. You can pay me whatever's on the meter. It ain't legal to bargain with a fare and don't tell me you don't know it!" He stabbed the starting button and wrenched the steering-wheel violently. Morgan clung to the arm-rest. The man gave him a rough ride over Wimbledon Common, dropped into the back reaches of Putney and skidded to the kerb. He turned with a wide grin.

"What number Ferndale was that again? It's gone clean out of my head."

Morgan answered steadily. Time was getting short. "Two-one-seven."

The driver managed to look as though he'd been asked to a leper colony. Ferndale ran parallel to the river, houses on one side, on the other a railed-off embankment. Shrouded cabin cruisers bobbed on the swollen water. The driver peered through the mist, his speed reduced to a crawl. Morgan rapped on the glass.

"Let me out here."

The man took his fare, refusing a tip. He sounded almost happy.

"Would you like my number now, *sir*?"

Morgan slammed the door. "Your face'll be enough to remember you by."

He bent his head into the rain, covering the last hundred yards at a jog-trot. The small apartment-house was covered with verbena vines. Water streamed from the guttering, dripped steadily on the steps leading up to the entrance hall. Upstairs someone was playing scales on a badly-tuned violin. He let himself into his flat and stood still in the darkness. Familiar sounds reassured him. He switched on the heater and draped his raincoat and trousers on a chair in front of it. The incident with the cab-driver disturbed him. Once again he'd shown bad judgement. He should be wearing anonymity like a skin — be the faceless head in the crowd — the man no one remembered.

The flat was small — bedroom, sitting-room, kitchen and bath. His mother's savings had furnished it. He had no feeling for comfort, accepting without interest the version of good taste supplied by the salesman. After four years, the veneer on the sharply-angled chairs had started to peel. He went into the kitchen. A neighbour's wife gave him an hour of her time daily, shopped for his modest needs. The usual sack of provisions was on the table, his laundry-basket on top of the refrigerator. He had changed his shirt and put on his trousers when a noise outside sent him to the light-switch. He threw it quickly and ran to the back door. He heard rain and rain and nothing else. He jerked the door open on a dismal stretch of garden. A line of garbage cans reached to the wall. The empty darkness dripped. He closed the door and started to fix himself a meal. The masseur was right—he was getting nervous.

Linda Swann

SHE woke with a start. The street lamp outside stretched fingers of light across the ceiling of the darkened room. She must have been sleeping for an hour—and dreaming. The images of childhood were still vaguely disturbing. The night-nursery where she huddled in a cocoon of blankets, listening to her father's slow tread along the corridor. The tall figure silhouetted against the bars of the fireguard. The smell of cologne. The ritual kiss and question. "*And has my girl been a good girl today?*"

Rain was tapping softly on the windowpanes. She lifted herself on an elbow, remembering Hugh's face as she had left the office. The barriers had been down and in that moment she had seen him clearly—scared and in desperate need. She understood why. The principles he lived by had been rejected for her sake. Her love for him welled, blind and uncomplicated. That he needed her mattered beyond anything else. She would be his strength.

She wrapped herself in a robe and drew the curtains. Rain, nostalgia, none of it was important any more. Neither tonight nor any other night. She was no longer alone. She switched on the heater, looking round the small room. There was little in it of her own. No photographs—no souvenirs. Nothing that reminded her of the past. She opened her wardrobe, making a face at what she saw there. She bought few clothes and Hugh knew every rag she owned. Today at least she should have made an effort, gone shopping instead of sleeping.

It was too late now. The stores would be closed. She'd have to do the best with what she had. She picked a high-necked sweater in soft black wool and a plain straight skirt, glad that her legs were good enough to make the most of. The streets would be filthy but the dirt would wipe off the glace kid shoes. She'd carry a spare pair of stockings in her handbag. She chose a darker lipstick than usual, a heavier liner for her eyes. She stepped back from the mirror, satisfied. This wasn't wishful thinking—she *was* younger, prettier and, yes, more desirable.

She sprayed her wrists and throat with the small bottle of Arpège and pinned the gilt brooch on her coat. Scent and brooch both Hugh's gifts. She glanced at the unmade bed, doubting that she'd sleep in it that night. Better that she left it as it was for Mrs. Burridge to find in the morning. The thought was strangely exciting—in a short while there'd be no need for this kind of subterfuge. She tried the sound over in her mind. "Mrs. Morgan. Mrs. *Linda* Morgan. Mrs. *Hugh* Morgan."

She was halfway through the door when she remembered the film. Her legs weakened as she looked for the shoulder-bag she used in the daytime. It was on the back of the chair, half-hidden by underclothing. She wrapped the phial in a wad of face-tissues, putting the whole thing in a folded office envelope. She locked her room and went down. Wet coats draped the hallstand. Four other girls roomed in the house. Other than by name she knew none of them. In the two years she'd lived there, only Mrs. Burridge had been beyond her doorstep. A pleasant-faced woman peered from the sittingroom as Linda reached the bottom of the stairs. Her white hair was piled on top of her head. Brass winked in the firelight behind her. A spaniel lay on its side facing the television set. The woman took off her spectacles, her manner surprised.

"Then you *were* in all that time, dear! How stupid of me. I knocked and knocked and couldn't get an answer."

Linda hooked her key on the board and turned. "I was tired, Mrs. Burridge. I think it's the weather. Anyway I slept for an hour. Don't worry about leaving the hall light on. I'm almost sure to be late."

33

The landlady wheedled the spaniel from the danger of its position near the fire and nodded.

"That's all right, dear. Do you want to leave a message in case he calls again?"

Linda's mouth thinned. This was the second time in a week that somebody had borrowed her umbrella. The insolence irritated her. She only half-took in what the other woman was saying as she searched for a replacement.

"It wasn't Mr. Morgan," the landlady said. "Someone else. A voice I don't know, dear. He sounded very mysterious -- wanting to know whether or not you were in. I said I thought I'd heard you earlier. I went up to make sure. I couldn't have been gone more than two minutes - when I came back down, the line was dead."

Linda was too shocked to reply for a moment. Then she faltered.

"But surely he left a name or a message?"

"Nothing." Mrs. Burridge said with a look of strong disapproval. "Yet he *sounded* a gentleman. It was a nice voice but not a *young* one, if you follow, dear."

Linda shivered. It was like being told a stranger had watched you undress. Just once, the brother of a girl she'd been at school with had telephoned her on his way home from Malaya. Apart from that, nobody but Hugh had ever called her at the house. She smiled with false understanding.

"I expect it was someone from the office. If he telephones again ask him to leave a message, Mrs. Burridge. Goodnight."

Rain and darkness hid the outlines of the shabby Victorian mansions outside. She walked rapidly towards the bus-stop, protecting her hair and makeup with the borrowed umbrella. There was a car parked beyond the third lamp-post. She looked at the two men sitting in the front seat without knowing why she did so. Their hats were tipped over their eyes as though they were sleeping. The one nearer her had folded his arms across his chest. She had a brief impression of a missing thumb and then she had passed.

She was lucky at the traffic-signals, boarding a half-empty bus on its last run back to the garage. The few passengers looked at her with disinterest as she found a seat halfway along the aisle. She held on tightly to her handbag, feeling the outline of the package inside through the thin leather. A quarter-of-a-mile on, three people hailed the bus. She stared at them blankly as they climbed aboard. A woman with a child and a sack of soaked groceries—a man in a trenchcoat and black Homburg hat. She watched his reflection in the steamed glass as he came down the aisle towards her. He sat on the opposite seat, two yards away. As he paid his fare she saw that the thumb on his right hand was missing. She started to tremble, waiting for him to show some sign of recognition. His pale blue eyes met hers without flickering. He merely nodded at the conductor and pulled a newspaper from his pocket. She rose quickly, stumbled along to the platform and punched the bell for the next stop. The top of Putney High Street showed through the slanting rain, five hundred yards away. She started to run, slipping on the wet sidewalk. Without turning her head she knew that the man in the trench-coat had dropped off the bus and was following her.

She pushed blindly through the crowds on the sidewalk, aware of the two constables standing in the shelter of a doorway, no longer able to ask their assistance. She'd crossed the line with Hugh that afternoon. She was convinced now that the phone call had been from someone Hugh sent to warn her—someone afraid to leave a name or message. Hugh had been tricked—the whole thing had been a trap to test his loyalty. The fake agent from a rival firm offering money for trade secrets that Faraday had allowed him to steal.

The film in her bag a magnet for people's eyes, she slowed to a saunter, realizing that haste was a sign of guilt. Without hint of what she was going to do, she ducked into the entrance to a movie-house. She'd bought her ticket and was into the darkened auditorium before her follower could have realized what had happened. She made her way straight to the far exit and rejoined Putney High Street two blocks up. There was no sign of the man in the black Homburg. The lights of the Cintra winked at the end of the arcade. She was no longer concerned for herself but for Hugh. To protect him she must be cunning and courageous.

It was a narrow room with a familiar face behind the bar. A middle-aged couple sat beneath a bullfight poster. Other than these three, the place was empty. She sat on a stool, untying her head-scarf and trying for an appearance of non-chalance. The mirrored shelves facing her reflected the length of the arcade. It was exactly nine o'clock. Hugh was never late. She had a picture of him sitting in a cell, convinced she had had his message and willing her to get rid of the film.

She was vaguely conscious of someone speaking to her. The barman was pointing at her fingers, smiling.

"You just lit that thing the wrong way up."

She thanked him, stubbing the smouldering filter into an ashtray. He snapped his lighter for her next cigarette.

"What can I get you to drink?"

She must have seen him a dozen times over the past two months. Ever since Hugh had started bringing her to the place. His accent was midway between Irish and American — Hugh said, Canadian. His brown hair was greying at the wings — his mouth firm and his eyes like those of a cat, unwavering and disconcerting.

"You want a drink or are you waiting?" he repeated.

She smiled at him nervously. "A sherry, please. A dry sherry. The man I come here with — have you seen him tonight?"

The barman shook his head with decision. "He's not been here since I came on duty and that's five o'clock."

Her arms stiffened as she looked into the mirror. The man in the Homburg hat had just turned into the entrance to the arcade. Another thirty yards and he'd be in the bar. She opened her handbag on impulse, dropping the squared envelope on the other side of the counter. She heard it fall on the floor. She spoke in a low desperate voice without turning her head.

"For God's sake, hide that! Don't give it back to anyone but me. I'll tell you why later."

What she would tell him she neither knew nor cared. For the moment she was safe. She watched him stoop, swiftly. His back straightened and he moved along the bar to greet the new customer. The envelope had vanished into the Canadian's hip-pocket. She sipped her sherry, glancing again covertly into the mirror. The stranger removed his trench-coat and hat and rested his elbows on the bar. Chin cupped in his palms, he considered the labels on the bottles. He looked set for an evening's drinking—a man sure of what he was about. Their eyes met briefly in reflection. She wondered whether she should flutter her lids—smile or something. Anything would be better than this awful uncertainty. He seemed to give her serious consideration for a moment and then turned away. The thumbless hand lifted his glass. She chilled again, thinking this was exactly how a detective *would* act.

She was aware that the Canadian was trying to attract her attention, leaning the top half of his body towards the entrance and nodding. She slid down from her stool and went to the door to meet Morgan. His hat and raincoat were saturated. He looked anxious and haggard. She helped him off with his coat, speaking in a low voice.

"The man sitting at the bar was outside the house in a car. He followed me here. Be careful."

Morgan blinked, greyfaced in the light, his thin smile showing the edge of his bridgework. He greeted her without fuss, leading her to a table at the far end of the bar. He sat down with his back to the man sitting on the stool. His expression changed.

"What do you mean, followed you?"

She told him the facts, conscious of his growing disbelief. The telling only confirmed her own opinions. The stranger was watching their every move.

Morgan moved his head impatiently. "Just give me the film, Linda. There's no time for hysterical nonsense. Nobody's been followed—nobody's in danger. Pass it over without making a production of it."

She reached across the table and imprisoned his hands in hers.

"Listen to me, Hugh. It's a trap and I'm sure of it. Even if it isn't, we don't *need* their money. We love one another— that's enough."

He freed his wrists slowly and deliberately. A sketchy shave had left specks of dried blood on his neck. His eyes were tired.

"I don't want to be unkind, Linda. Neither of us is used to this sort of thing. But we've come too far to turn back. Give me the film."

She knew then that she couldn't tell him the truth. Something had happened to him since this afternoon—the change driving him beyond the limits of sense and caution. He was obsessed with his theft and what it meant to them.

"I didn't bring it," she lied. "I've been terrified ever since that man telephoned the house tonight. I left it behind."

His easy smile died as he heard the news. He picked up his hat and coat.

"Get your things. We're going back to the house."

She stood near the entrance, refusing to look as he stood by the bar, telephoning for a cab. She noticed that as they walked out, the man in the Homburg was paying his bill. They were silent in the taxi, each preoccupied with personal thoughts. She glanced at him once under lowered lids. His face had the same tenseness that had worried her ever since he'd confessed. He stopped the driver a half-block from her house. They took refuge in a neighbouring driveway as the man reversed and drove off. His headlamps picked out a car parked further up under the dripping trees. She recognized its shape and colour and grabbed Morgan's arm.

"It's the same car, Hugh—the one I saw earlier. We didn't pass it on the way home. They must have followed us."

He took her by the shoulders, screwing his thumbs into her flesh until she thought she must scream. The pain

38

stopped as he released her. He wiped his forehead, his voice jerky like a man come to his last argument.

"You've got to stop it, Linda: Do you hear—you must stop it! That car is empty—nobody has followed you. *The —car—is empty!*" he emphasized.

She carried his hands to her shoulders, shaking her head obstinately.

"And what about the telephone call—did Mrs. Burridge invent that? And the man in that bar—I saw the way you looked at him, Hugh."

His hands lifted in resignation. "Because you were acting like someone in a Hitchcock movie. An insurance agent—a bank clerk—who the hell knows! He's home and in bed by now if he's got any sense. Where I should be. Go in and get the film, Linda."

She crossed the road and used her key as quietly as she could. The light was still burning in the hallway. She looked at the familiar objects with quiet desperation, wondering what came next. The wet coats were still there, their owners upstairs drinking hot milk and swapping hair-curlers. There were thousands of names and addresses in the telephone directory—and not one she could call for help. She unhooked her key and crept upstairs carrying her shoes in her hand. Her room unlocked, she went to the window. The car was still parked in the same position, apparently unattended. Hugh had to be hiding in the trees. She slumped on the bed in the darkness. After a while she struck a match. The minutes had to be passed, dimensions given to the lie she was going to tell. She smoked without tasting the tobacco, indifferent to the tears ruining her make-up. She had the feeling that something terrible was going to happen—something that she could do nothing to stop. She sponged her eyes with cold water and did what she could with her lipstick. It would be too dark for him to see the mess her face was in.

Televised drama was strident from behind Mrs. Burridge's door. Linda let herself out quietly. Morgan came from the trees by the gate. There was enough light from the street-lamp for her to see the relieved face behind the outstretched hand. She shook her head, knowing that in a second he would be aloof and accusing.

"I can't get at it, Hugh. I put it in the downstairs linen cupboard. Mrs. Burridge has locked up for the night."

His smile changed to an expression of shocked disbelief. "What the hell do you mean 'locked-up'?"

His mouth was ugly. She avoided looking at it. "The linen cupboard's through the kitchen. She locks everything downstairs before she goes to bed."

He took her by the arms, staring into her eyes, his voice very quiet.

"We're in this together, Linda. That's something you'd better get into your head very clearly. A lie can finish us."

Somehow she managed to sound convincing. "I'm not lying, Hugh."

He let her go, his manner suddenly remote. "No. No. of course not, darling. What time does she unlock in the morning?"

She took a deep breath. "About half-past-seven. It depends how late she goes to bed."

"Can't you think of an excuse to get her to open up tonight? Surely you can say that you've left something."

"To start with, I've no reason to be in her part of the house," she said firmly. "There's nothing I can do till the morning."

After a moment's reflection, he raised his shoulders. "It'll have to be like that, then. Get busy just as soon as you hear her move. Take a taxi to my place, I'll be waiting for you. We can have breakfast together and then go on to work." He bent down, framing her face in his hands. "Everything depends on you now, Linda. *Everything*."

She turned away, holding the touch of his mouth against her cheek. She hurried back to her room and watched him from her window. He was a thin, shabby figure hugging the wall. He forked left at the traffic-signals and was lost to her sight. She moved her eyes to the parked car beyond the street-lamp, fighting the fluttering in her stomach. A door slammed. Headlights blazed and then dipped twice before the car was driven off at high speed.

Fresh tears forced their way past tightly-shut eyelids. She had asked for trust and repaid it with deception. She pulled herself together and collected her things. Mrs. Burridge's television set was still playing as Linda left the house. She stopped the bus at Putney Bridge and turned south. The crowds had thinned. Cars swooshed by on the wet tarmac, spraying the sidewalks. She climbed the hill, muffled in her coat-collar, her reflection following her in endless shop-windows. For the moment her brain was numbed to danger. She no longer looked behind her — no longer tried to remember how to pray — but walked like a woman in her sleep, removed from reality.

The Cintra sign blinked at the end of the arcade. She paused outside the door, looking in. Voices drowned the taped flamenco music. The room was filled with youngsters groomed to razor-sharp smartness. Their girls milled about with an air of pert sophistication, wearing long straight hair and suede jackets. The men stood in restless groups, ignoring one another pointedly.

She made her way through the throng, excusing herself nervously. A smell of implicit violence hung like pepper in the air. She had only read about such people. Newspapers reported their activities daily. Rival factions of teenagers who moved into bar or pub, taking it over entirely for the length of their stay. They defied any authority not backed by force. The only customers who stayed were those with strong nerves. Being in a room with them was like sitting on sticks of gelignite, fused and ready to blow. A word, look or gesture could provide the spark, turning an orderly bar into a nightmare of shrieking hoodlums armed with bicycle-chains and knives. Sometimes the scene was played in restrained fashion, the actors contenting themselves with a parade of mutual contempt. The gamble kept inn-keepers wary-eyed and with a hand close to the phone.

She found a stool at the bar. Two people were serving

drinks. A ferretfaced redhead in a white jacket and the ex-fighter she remembered as the proprietor. A police-whistle dangled ostentatiously from a cord round his wrist. A heavy wooden hammer was propped on the shelf behind him. Both men were sweating heavily. She bought herself a brandy, not caring that she hadn't eaten. A quarter-hour passed without sign of the Canadian. She drew the attention of the redheaded barman. He came towards her grinning in a way that made her skin crawl. Pale-blue eyes settled on her breasts.

She controlled herself with an effort. "Do you mind telling the other barman that I'd like to speak to him?"

He showed small pointed teeth like a cat's and winked. "You don't want to worry about him, dear. He's just a low common fellow. Why don't you try me?"

Her voice started to shake with anger. "I'll keep it in mind. Whenever the drains need attention."

He let the match in his fingers die, then flicked his hand thoughtfully.

"That's not the way to make me show willing, is it, now, dear?"

"Just do as you're told," she said steadily.

He gave the bar a perfunctory wipe with a rag. "Of course, miss. Well now, it so happens that your friend has gone home. If you hurry you just might catch him before he gets his burglar's tools out. But make it snappy, once he's about he's a will-of-the-wisp."

There was a sudden surge in the bar before she could answer. The groups of teenagers split into pairs and three-somes and walked sedately into the arcade. As they came to the street, they turned bland, disinterested faces on the police-car waiting for them. Henschel wasted no time duck-ing under the bar and bolting the door. He came back blow-ing hard and poured himself a large belt of scotch. He lowered it at a swallow and addressed the room in general.

"The bastards! 'Society's problem', shit! What makes 'em any different from what we were as kids? I'll tell you—nobody lifts a hand to them. The law's as bad—these bastards can break a man's place up and if you touch one of 'em you're in dead trouble. What are *you* looking at?" he finished morosely.

The redhead cleared his throat ostentatiously. "This lady wants Duncan's address, Sam. She's a friend of his, she says."

Henschel swivelled his heavy body. Eyes sunk deep in pads of putty-coloured flesh considered her sombrely. He nodded tardy recognition.

"Good evening, miss. What's the trouble?"

She made a quick gesture of dissent. "There's no trouble at all. It's just that I have to see him urgently about something."

Henschel emptied his glass again and wiped his mouth with thick fingers. His voice stumbled over the difficult syllables. The sense of what he was trying to say seemed to evade him.

"Then that's all right, isn't it, miss. As long as a man does his job, I don't give a bugger—beg pardon—I don't . . . it don't matter to me whether he comes from the nick or a Sunday school. *All* my customers are entitled to a fair measure and the right change—even that shower that just left. But what happens off the premises is no responsibility of mine. None *what-so-ever*." He poured himself another generous drink.

She climbed down from her stool, hoping her legs wouldn't fail. She was beginning to feel slightly sick again. The man was drunk but she had to understand him. She smiled painfully.

"I don't blame you for thinking it odd, me coming here at this time at night. It's just that I have to see Mr. Duncan urgently on a matter that's personal." Both men looked at her speculatively. She felt her cheeks colour.

Henschel spoke to the redhead. "Get the outside lights off. You can start clearing up. I've had enough for one night." He rang the cash-register, scooped the contents of the drawers into the pockets of his windbreaker. He belched twice, frowning at his reflection in the glass and came back to where she was standing. He looked at her unsteadily.

"You're a customer, miss. You come in here asking for one of my barmen's address. But no trouble, you say. That's fair enough. Duncan minds his own business. He don't steal —at least not from me. I ain't going to give you his address and do you know why—because I don't know it. What's more, I doubt if anyone else does either."

The arcade was suddenly dark as the barman cut the lights. He came back and started piling the chairs on top of the tables. She fastened her coat self-consciously. Her voice was no more than a whisper.

"Will he be here tomorrow?"

Henschel yawned, exposing black teeth stained with tobacco.

"Half-past-eleven. Don't worry, miss. It may never happen." He turned the yawn into a smile.

She picked up her handbag from the stool and left the bar without looking back. She was dimly aware of passing bus-stops and roving cabs but knew only that she must keep walking. On past the furtive whispers of solitary men, the banal compliments and wolf-whistles. It was three-quarters of an hour later that she turned by the traffic-signals at the bottom of her street. She had tried to call Hugh twice on the way home. That had been her first impulse—to run to him and explain how one lie had demanded its successors. His number had rung unanswered. There was no telling at what time he would return. She had no key to his apartment and no heart to face him again that night. This was the real truth. She had no heart to reveal her treachery.

Mrs. Burridge had taken her at her word. The house was in complete darkness. She felt her way up the stairs and into her room. She undressed without turning on the light, crawled into bed and wrapped herself in the bedclothes. It seemed an eternity since she had awakened that evening, excited and hopeful. She burrowed her face still deeper into the pillows, shaken by the violence of uncontrollable sobbing. After a while, she slept.

Hugh Morgan

LIGHTS spanned the bridge ahead. He started to walk to the north side of the river as the church clock pealed the hour. The bridge was deserted but he put himself on show under a lamp-post. Seconds later, a black Humber appeared coming from the Putney shore. The driver bleeped his horn twice. Morgan walked back to meet the car. The near front door was already unlatched. Before he had both feet off the sidewalk, the driver let in his clutch. The man had a young set face under yellowish hair. A rugby-scarf was wound round his throat. He kept his mouth closed and his eyes on the road. The radio was beamed to a programme of dance-music.

"Turn that thing off."

Morgan swung round towards the rear seat, recognizing the accent. Ashe was sitting in the attitude of a Japanese wrestler, feet flat on the floor, hands on his knees with his elbows sticking out. The driver killed the music. The low hum of the motor dominated the silence. Morgan laid his arm along the back of the seat, focusing on Ashe's face.

"I haven't got it," he said quickly. He sensed their unspoken communication. His tension increased. He started to bluster. "I haven't brought it for a good reason. It's under lock and key for the night. You can have it any time after eight in the morning."

"And the girl?" Ashe's enquiry was almost tender.

"At home—*her* home."

Ashe showed no sign of having heard but said something to the driver. A rattle of consonants that meant nothing to Morgan. The car veered left off the main road, gunned a hundred yards between blank walls and swung to the kerb. The wipers swished on, sweeping arcs of rain from the wind-

his neck under his right ear. He made an involuntary move-ment with his hand then gasped as the driver struck vici-ously with the bunch of keys. Morgan held himself upright on clenched fists, fighting the pain in his wrist.

Ashe's voice was harsh with warning. "I'll blow your head open if I have to. You're going for a nice quiet ride with friends. Whenever we stop, remember to act like it."

The driver set the Humber in motion. He drove like an expert, using brakes and motor without drawing attention to his speed. He avoided the main thoroughfares, cutting through the back-doubles. Morgan was in the same stilted position. A dead stub stuck to his bottom lip. He dared not remove it. The cross-country route baffled him but after half-an-hour of it, the treelined slopes and decorous gen-tility of the houses gave him a clue. They were somewhere in the south-eastern suburbs—Dulwich or Sydenham. The car slowed at the bottom of a dark avenue. He sensed Ashe's movement from behind but made no attempt to block it. A towel was pulled over his head and held at the nape of his neck. The rough fabric stank of oil. He saw nothing. He swayed as the car turned into a driveway. The noise of tyres on gravel was unmistakable. The car stopped. Ashe whipped the towel off taking the cigarette-stub with it.

"Out," he said curtly.

The driver closed heavy gates on the cobbled yard. The first-floor windows of house and outbuildings were protected with iron bars. Wind whipped through the cowled chimney-pots setting up a racket like a football rattle. A dog barked somewhere inside. Ashe opened a back door. The driver propelled Morgan along the corridor using his weight as if he enjoyed it. A final shove sent Morgan sprawling at the bottom of the stairs. The planes of the blond's face were flat under the hundred watt lamp, his eyes pinpoints of animosity. He shifted his weight from one foot to the other and cracked his knuckles.

"Get up those stairs!"

Morgan pushed the baize door at the top. He crossed a hall papered in dull red and walked through the open door.

A fire burnt brightly on a combination of comfort and disorder. Books and magazines lay where the reader had abandoned them. A claw-footed desk was littered with birdprints, a plate of bread-and-butter and a china pot of Stilton. A hi-fi set was playing Berlioz beyond the closed dividing doors. It was the kind of room Morgan despised. Because of it, he mistrusted its owner on sight.

The man was inches over six feet but bent from the hips. He had a large bald head and questing nose. Ringed eyes and tufted brows completed the impression of a bird of prey. He was wearing soft tweeds woven in herringbone pattern, a flannel shirt and homespun tie. He lifted a pipe covered in leather.

"Sit down, please, Mr. Morgan."

A parchment lamp was tilted so that its light shone directly on the tapestry chair. As Morgan sat down, a yellow-eyed collie dropped its tail and slunk off, grumbling in its throat. The man who had driven the car was sitting at the shadowed end of the room, silent and watchful. The tall man moved in front of the fire and splayed his legs. Morgan raised his head and laughed nervously.

"You're putting on a very unsubtle performance. We're not adolescents."

The tall man spoke as though he enjoyed the sound of words. "The virtue of subtlety lies in the ability to implement it with force. That I can do."

The dog growled from beneath the table as Morgan shifted his chair deliberately. The light no longer shone in his eyes.

"That sounds far too much like a threat for me to appreciate it."

The man waved acknowledgement with his pipe. "I wouldn't have thought so. Excess of zeal, possibly—nothing more. It's an odd thing—everything I know about you seems to be in contradiction to events. Or perhaps not so odd—life often *is* like that, isn't it? I'd like you to tell me what happened to the latest information on Project Lederle."

They lived well, these intrepid fighters for freedom—in

warm comfort surrounded by animals and—he'd heard the voices beyond the dividing-doors—a woman or two. Beautiful, of course, sweet-smelling and skilled in dialectics. The shabbiness of his own appearance made him answer impulsively.

"I'd like you to remember something. I'm a worker not a university sympathizer. I've risked everything I've got for an ideal on five different occasions. I'm ready to do it again. But I don't like threats."

The cultured voice was full of concern. "I thought we were talking about the Lederle film. But if you'd rather not . . ." he spread his hands with gentle irony.

"I haven't finished what I wanted to say," Morgan said doggedly. "I was born in a slum. My mother cleaned out other people's lavatories—ate their leavings—to shove me one rung up on the ladder. My birth-certificate says 'Father unknown.' I've been a Marxist ever since I was old enough to understand why these things could happen to me and not to others. Since I understood a system that prostitutes man's spirit and hopes."

The tall man smiled politely. "It's a stirring denunciation but not entirely true. Your resentment at established order stems from an entirely different motive. You're first and foremost a seeker after personal power. Not that that matters as long as it can be controlled. So far your contributions to the cause have outweighed your lack of idealism. Do I make myself quite clear?"

Morgan's fingers found his wrist. The vicious blow with the keys had left the flesh bruised and swollen. He was uncertain what he was being accused of. In spite of himself, his voice broke.

" 'Lack of idealism'?"

The tall man sauntered to the desk. He cut himself a wafer of bread, folded it fastidiously so that neither butter nor Stilton touched his fingers. He popped the morsel into his mouth which he wiped with a maroon silk handkerchief.

"This girl," he said clearly. "I want to know how she

comes to be connected with the film. I'm sure there's a reason. I'd like to hear it."

Morgan looked at him without understanding. That this sort of thing happened, he'd always known. But never to him. As long as they'd worked, no one had ever queried his methods. He started to explain in a dull monotone. The pipesmoker listened carefully, interrupting once to apologize for throwing fuel on the fire. He blew flame with a pair of bellows. When Morgan was done, his interrogator straightened his long back.

"The heart of the matter is that this girl's had the film in her possession since half-past-four this afternoon. For all we know, it could be sitting on a desk in Scotland Yard."

Morgan's protest was despairing. 'That's ridiculous. Do you think I'd be sitting here if that were possible. I value my liberty as much as anyone. No matter who says anything to the contrary, I'm as certain of this girl as I am of life itself."

The tall man's smile was always courteous, sometimes gentle. As if the memories of many pleasant things blotted out the exigencies of the moment. He held the door open for the whining collie and watched it solicitously across the hall. He swung round. "I ought to tell you this, I believe you—I believe that we'll have this film in our possession tomorrow, Mr. Morgan. In spite of what is certainly bad judgement on your part. You're an essential part of a concerted effort. That's why we must both make allowances— both continue the struggle. You're job's not finished. You won't see Miss Swann again," he said casually and scratched his shoulder-blade against the mantel.

Morgan's relief was tinged with doubt. "She's bringing the film to my flat first thing in the morning."

His interrogator knocked his pipe into the hearth, cocking his head as if he heard something beyond the immediate sounds.

"You won't see her again," he repeated. His quiet voice was uncompromisingly final. "Someone will telephone your office in the morning speaking on behalf of Miss Swann.

She'll be taking a few days off. What's your normal procedure in a case like that?"

Morgan came to his feet slowly—careful not to make the sort of move that would disturb the man still sitting in the shadows.

"I'd send the message over to *Personnel*. They'd see I got someone from the typist pool. Officially that should be the end of it. But after yesterday's interview, I think Sangster might want to see me."

The tall man crammed fresh tobacco in the bowl of his pipe. He used the intervals between sucking and blowing to expound.

"That's precisely what I'm counting on him to do. You'll have a letter some time tomorrow—a typewritten letter signed by the girl. The signature will be genuine. Keep it for the coroner's inquest. And don't worry—it won't be the first time an impressionable woman's made a fool of herself over a man. Nobody thinks the worse of him."

Morgan's respect was ungrudging. This man really understood.

"She uses sleeping-pills," he said huskily. He cleared his throat suddenly aware of the blond's peculiar stare. "I don't know what brand."

The ringed eyes were hooded in crepe-like lids and rarely blinked.

"Don't bother your head about it. Go to work in the same way as usual and make no contacts at all. We'll get in touch with you. Henry will drive you home. Good night."

Morgan followed the blond across the hall and down the stairs. The man stopped in the passageway, turned and put his face to Morgan's.

"You and your bloody mother," he said savagely. "What are you looking for—someone to kiss you good night?"

Linda Swann

SHE closed her room as quietly as she could and tiptoed down the stairs. Someone was using the bathroom on the floor above. The rest of the house still slept. She unbolted the front door and picked the letters off the mat. She extracted the one envelope that was addressed to her. The name of the sender was printed on the outside. Goodge & Collins, Insurance Brokers. She put it in her bag unopened. Who else did she expect would be writing to her? There were no Swanns left nearer than New Zealand. The English cousins she had dropped years ago. It had used to be Hugh she hoped would write to her--the wish had become an obsession this last year at Faraday's. It wasn't that they hadn't been close. She had slept with him. Some men might be able to do that without loving but not Hugh. He was simply afraid to put love into words—terrified of being hurt. And, dear God, she knew all about that. But there was much more to it. He was bitter about things that didn't matter. He remembered a childhood passed in mean back streets so vividly that her own memories became somehow false and pretentious. It was all so desperately wrong. Hugh had more to offer than any other man she had ever met. He had proved it without putting words on paper.

The long restless night had darkened the hollows under her eyes but she felt alive and happy. No matter what he decided they must do about the film, they would do it together. From now on there'd be no lies between them.

She opened the street door. Weeds grew from the cracks in the asphalt driveway. The patch of grass was muddied and ugly with litter. But the elm branches glistened in the early-morning sunshine. She picked her way across the path. The chow from further down the street was stalking the postman. A smell of bacon frying came from the neighbouring house.

It was difficult to believe in anything that had happened the night before. She looked at her watch. It was almost half-past-seven.

Chances of finding a cab were doubled if she walked as far as the traffic-signals. The next hour wasn't going to be easy but the prospect of facing Hugh was less frightening than it had been. There was something horrible about admitting that you'd deceived a person who loved you but a man like Hugh would understand. She'd take the morning off and be at the bar when the Canadian arrived. With any luck he'd be by himself. She tried a couple of easy phrases in her head and then gave up. Hugh would tell her what to say. She was a hundred yards away from the junction when a black car slid alongside and stopped at the kerb. A man jumped out briskly from the back and put himself squarely in her path. He wore a dark grey suit and elastic-sided boots and looked like a farmer.

"Are you Miss Swann—Miss Linda Swann?"

She stopped dead, clutching her bag to her chest. "That's right," she faltered.

He opened his palm on a small oblong folder. "Police-officers. You'll have to come with us."

He had a harsh, peculiar accent that she was unable to place. There was nothing complicated about his manner however. He grabbed her elbow firmly and assisted her into the car. She sat next to him, hands clasped demurely in her lap, ankles crossed. "Linda Swann" he had said but this was happening to someone entirely different. A stranger. The driver let in his clutch and the big car glided as far as the signals then stopped. People were waiting on both sides of the street at the bus-stop—talking, reading newspapers. The butcher was hosing down his steps. A garbage-truck was backed up by the pub on the corner. She noticed with interest that the men working on it wore black coats with white patches and gloves. She wondered why white gloves.

The detective beside her sharpened his voice. "You've been a very silly young lady, haven't you?"

She took a moment to consider what she thought he meant.

She looked guilty of anything and knew it. There was sweat on her upper lip and she was on the verge of the shakes. She remembered that they were trained to record and weigh every gesture she made—every nuance of her speech. They must have arrested Hugh already. That much was certain. But they still had to have proof. She knew instinctively that Hugh would tell them nothing and that he would expect her to do the same. She must ask for a lawyer. There was enough money in the bank to pay for a good one. She had the feeling that this was what they would need. She answered him coolly.

"I'm quite sure you're used to hearing this sort of thing but I honestly haven't the first idea what you're talking about." She took the cigarette and light that he offered her—held the first inhalation in her empty stomach till giddiness set in.

He removed his hat and put it down on the seat between them. A bone-white ragged scar ran the length of his skull, only partly concealed by his hair. He clucked regretfully.

"That's not true, is it, Miss? You've got a film in your possession—a film containing classified information, the property of Faraday Electronic Research Company and Her Majesty's Government. We know how and where you obtained this film but for the moment that's secondary. Our chief concern is to see that this information doesn't reach the wrong hands. Do you mind giving me your bag?"

She smiled shakily. "Not at all." They did this in movies —*"Now think carefully, Miss Swann! Where were you on the night of the fifth?"*

He dumped the contents of the bag into his lap and made a thorough inspection. The driver was whistling through his teeth softly. Occasionally his eyes met hers in the mirror but he never opened his mouth. They were travelling fast now, avoiding the first rush of the morning traffic.

"I haven't the first idea what you're talking about," she repeated stubbornly.

He shrugged heavy shoulders. Before she could stop him, his fingers were probing the lining of her coat, her collar.

She froze as he touched her body intimately. He let her go, his tone considerably sharper.

"Very well, Miss Swann, you'll be searched later. You're taking the wrong attitude, you know. Morgan hasn't been worrying about you. How do you suppose that we knew that you had the film? No, he realizes that you're both in serious trouble and is sensible enough to want to get out of it. It's entirely up to you whether or not the two of you finish in jail. We're principally interested in returning the film. The rest is for other authorities to decide. Between you and me cooperation will do a lot for you."

It was a trick. She had read about it, heard about it, a hundred times. This was the way detectives worked—turning one suspect against another. If Hugh *had* talked, they wouldn't be here, these men. They'd be back at the house, tearing Mrs. Burridge's kitchen apart. She had a quick sense of triumph. Even if they did search they would find nothing and it would be her lies that finally saved Hugh. She tried hard to remember whether there was anything in her room to connect her with the *Cintra*. There couldn't be. No one in the bar even knew her name. The barman would probably push the envelope into a drawer and forget about it. If he opened it, what would it mean—nothing.

"Tell me, Sergeant—or is it Inspector—does the law say I have to answer these questions? Isn't there something about a caution first?"

She had the distinct impression that the remark disturbed him.

"That's up to you," he replied. "And it's Inspector."

She pitched the cigarette through the window. "Then I've nothing to say."

They stopped at a busy intersection. She could no longer recognize the streets or buildings but the postal number told her that they were in the south-east suburbs. The car hummed up a long incline, traversing quiet roads where children played tag on their way to school. Men in striped aprons delivered milk, their breath vaporous in the raw air. Painted gates flicked past Charles Addams houses, dark rambling and forbidding. The car turned onto a gravelled driveway and ghosted between dense banks of untrimmed laurel.

She started to shake violently. "This isn't a police-station!" She tried to scream but her voice cracked.

The man sitting next to her moved like a conjuror. She stared at the automatic in his hand with disbelief. The barrel pointed directly at her stomach. His mouth and eyes were hostile.

"Shut up and do as you're told."

They circled a lawn spiked with croquet hoops and stopped in a cobbled yard. A dog barked in the house. The driver swung round in his seat, shoving a hand through his springy blond hair.

"If you know what's good for you," he added, smiling. Something about the way he spoke reminded her of Hugh when he was being derisive about what he called his Polytechnic accent.

The other man was waiting at one of the back doors. She saw the curtain move at the window, took a few steps towards him and whirled, running for the avenue of laurels. The driver loped after her easily, grabbing her by the shoulder before she had covered a dozen yards. He wrenched her bag away and tossed it to his companion. Then he locked her arms tight behind her back, lifted and rushed her across the yard into the house. He followed her along the passage, pushing her roughly up the short flight of stairs into a hall. He yelled to someone out of sight as she flattened herself against the wall. The house seemed full of voices. There was a dragging sound from below — as if a heavy weight were being dragged across the wooden flooring. The dog set up a sort of howling in the distance. The man shut the door and pointed.

"Leave your shoes down here and get upstairs."

She placed the saddlestitched loafers neatly side by side, looking for an open door or window. He jerked his head impatiently. She went up in front of him, her stockinged feet soundless on the blue carpeting. She stopped at the head of the staircase waiting for his directions. Red and crimson flower-paintings glowed against the cream walls on the landing. He pushed by and turned the handle on a large bathroom. The oversized tub, the wall-to-wall carpet and curtains were of the same warm pink. Angled mirrors backed a long dressing-table whose glass top was littered with bottles. .An electric shaver was still plugged in its socket. A sun-lamp dangled over a rowing-machine that was bolted to the floor. She stood in the centre of the room, watching his expression apprehensively. He averted his gaze, his voice embarrassed.

"Take your clothes off!"

He went out, taking the key with him. She ran to the window. A catch operated a central locking device. Down below, dahlias bloomed in a bed of soft earth. She unfastened the catch and wrenched the window open. She was sitting on the sill with her legs dangling outside when the bathroom door opened. A woman came forward unhurriedly, smiling. Her ash-blonde hair was looped and plaited over a wide forehead. Her voice was friendly and soothing.

"Now get back inside. You're almost certain to break something and it's no good anyway."

She put her head out of the window and called. The blonde's head appeared from the room below. He looked up, grinning and waved a hand. Linda swung her legs back into the bathroom. The woman made no attempt to touch her but stood in front of the mirror, repinning a strand of pale hair.

"Sometimes I wish I could wear it long like you," she said conversationally. "But I'm too old."

Linda lowered her feet to the ground and caught the woman's hand. The third finger wore a plain gold band.

"Help me," she pleaded. 'You must help me."

The woman smiled like a nurse admonishing a patient. "But that's exactly what we're trying to do, you silly girl. Now shut the window or you'll catch your death of cold. Take your clothes off—there's absolutely nothing to be afraid of, Linda." She unfastened a linen-closet and draped a towelling robe over Linda's arm.

She unzipped her skirt mechanically and stepped out of

it. She let each garment fall at the other woman's feet till finally she stood naked. The warm robe smelled of lavender. She watched the capable fingers explore every possible hiding-place in her clothing.

"All right, dear. You can put your things on again now." The woman's voice had a throaty quality. Her accent, like her clothes, was good-class and unpretentious. She was handsome in Baltic fashion, wide through the cheekbones with eyes the colour of bruised violets. She looked speculatively as Linda pulled on her garter-belt. The quiet comforting manner, the constant use of her first name—all these smacked of the false friendliness of the police investigator. Yet these people certainly *weren't* the police. Her mind sought an alternative.

"Wouldn't you like to do your hair?" The woman was offering an ivory-backed brush.

Linda took it guardedly. An idea was slowly forming—an idea that would account for her abduction and for these people. They represented Faraday's competitor's—this French firm Hugh was selling information to. Suppose they'd already parted with the money—they'd think Hugh was trying to swindle them. She had the impression that people like this would stop at nothing.

Her hair crackled under the steady strokes of her wrist. She gave the brush back, thanking the woman politely. They stood for a second, watching one another intently. Linda's words came with a rush.

"Please let me see Hugh—*please!*"

The woman moved as far as the door. "Downstairs now, dear. You can leave your bag up here—you'll be coming back."

Linda hurried down the stairs, crossing the hall sure that Hugh would be waiting. Possibly a prisoner like herself but *there*. His face would tell her what to do. She came into the room, with a strong sense of *déja-vu*—she felt that she already knew every inch of its shabby comfort. The sagging chairs smelling of leather-polish, the disarray of magazines, the brick fireplace with its smoky mantelpiece. She sat down, looking doubtfully at the man in front of the fire. In that first instant, she saw him as a great bird unfolding its wings for flight. He glanced quickly at the woman who had searched Linda. She shook her head and went out, shutting the door after her. The man's voice was deep and soothing.

"Now you mustn't be frightened, Linda. Frightened people find it difficult to apply reason and that's what we have to do, isn't it?"

She looked down at her stockinged feet. His eyes troubled her. They were without depth, the pupils ringed and had none of the concern that sounded in his voice. She held on tightly to her shaking wrists, concealing the crisscross of scars. He came over to her and raised her chin, forced her to meet his searching gaze. The smell of his fingers was a link with her childhood. A bedroom in semi-darkness, a feeling of intense heat and continued thirst—someone else's hand, cool on her brow.

She spoke with absolute certainty. "You're a doctor, aren't you?"

He went back to the fireplace. Still the great bird but now hooded.

"It's just possible that you *are* telling the truth. There's a simple way of proving it. I'd like you to tell me exactly what happened to you since half-past-four yesterday afternoon. Leave out nothing. Where you went—who you saw—who you spoke to. Have you had any breakfast yet?"

She stared carefully into the fire. The ends of his stethoscope had been tucked out of sight.

She answered in a dull, hopeless voice. "No."

He opened the door and called down the service stairs. He came back smiling.

"They'll bring something up. Tell me what happened. If it's the truth, I promise I'll help you."

She sat with slumped shoulders looking at the pattern of the carpet, the creeping flames, at anything but the ringed eyes with nothing behind them. It was simple for her to lie. All she did was forget the film.

He let her talk without hindrance, taking the tray from the woman and placing it on the table at Linda's side. He poured the coffee for her. There were hot rolls, butter and marmalade under the napkin. She ate and drank gratefully. He hooked his heels over the fender.

"And that's everything is it, Linda?"

"Everything," she said firmly.

He shook his head disappointedly. "You start work at half-past nine. It takes twenty minutes to reach Faraday's from your house, half-an-hour at most. What were you doing wandering about the streets just after seven?"

"I was going to Mr. Morgan's," she said steadily. "For breakfast."

He thought about this for a moment. "I see. He says he gave you this film. Why do you think he's lying, Linda?"

She spread her hands. "I can't believe that he did say it. Why don't you let me see him?"

He shifted a soapstone figurine along the mantelpiece, frowning.

"A man telephoned your house last night and left no name. Another man followed you to this bar in Putney. You knew both these things but didn't mention them. Why?"

Her answer was barely audible. "I was afraid."

His hand stabbed accusation. "The film was never left in the house, was it, Linda? You passed it on to someone else but who?" He snapped thumb against finger, his face suddenly serene. "The man in the bar, of course! It was someone in the bar, wasn't it?"

She buried her face in her hands, shutting out the sound of his voice. When she finally undid her fingers, she was alone in the room. The woman spoke pleasantly from the doorway.

"Come along, Linda. We'll go upstairs. You can lie down and rest. It'll do you the world of good."

Linda shook her head. "Please let me go! They'll be looking for me soon. If you let me go I swear I won't say a thing to anyone."

The woman came over holding out both hands. They touched Linda's shoulders gently but firmly.

"Come along, dear," she said quietly. "I'll find you some pyjamas."

Ritchie Duncan

HE made breakfast the quick, forbidden way. The electric ring coupled to the light-socket, Nescafé, a pair of bananas. Done with it, he looked down at the street. Last night's rain had dispersed the fog. The buildings and pavements glistened with the raw promise of harsher weather. Tyres left their tracks in the hoar frost. People walked heavily muffled. He turned away from the window, yawning.

He'd slept badly as he always did when his routine was disturbed by the split-shift. He counted last night's tips. A lousy twelve bob. He'd been back in the stockroom when that redheaded bastard had emptied the box. He was certain the guy was holding out on him. There'd been a stream of good spenders in during the afternoon.

He picked out a couple of coins, yawning again. The rest of the money went into his suitcase. He locked this and hid the key under the bed. He'd saved ninety pounds in ten weeks. Another two months with Christmas coming should about do it. Henschel had promised a bonus if he worked through the holidays. And why not—what the hell else would he do.

He shaved, thinking about Christmas at Duncan's Reach. First had come breakfast—the porridge served on ceremonial silver. Then the long walk to church across paddocks hock-deep in old snow. Home again to the excitement of rooms filled with wrapped gifts and leaping firelight. One o'clock and Baxter in a striped waistcoat beating the dinner-gong, pop-eyed in anticipation of the coming champagne. The dinner-table with eleven bowed heads, behind them the sober faces of the servants. And at the head of the table, God in a kilt. His grandfather's blessing and prayers were immutable.

". . . and now God the Father . . ." Eleven heads lifted cautiously. He caught his sister's furtive wink. His grandfather's voice droned on. ". . . . our ancestors came from twilight into night, dispossessed and exiled to a foreign land they made their own. With the help of the Almighty they prospered and so there was morning." Eleven hands clutched glasses in readiness for the barked command. "The King, God bless him!" He still remembered the tang of bubbles exploding in his nose as he drank the health of a Bavarian prince in the name of the Stuarts.

He wiped his razor and dressed. He was almost out of the room when he saw the paper sticking out of the vase. He walked back and picked it up. The shape of the cylinder inside was too thick for it to be a lipstick. More likely a pair of nylon briefs. He'd seen them packaged in such containers. The thought amused him. She hadn't looked the type, somehow. More like lace. His smile faded as he recalled her strained face, the jumpiness underlying her parade of nonchalance. For some reason or other the girl had been truly scared. He pushed the envelope into a pocket. She'd be back with the answer.

Across the landing, Plotkin was banging on his typewriter. Plotkin—import and export—hawking Japanese cherubs to hang on plastic Christmas trees. Duncan closed the street door and caught a bus on the corner. He let himself off at Putney Bridge and started up the long drag to the *Cintra*. He was halfway down the arcade when he saw that the bar doors were open. His first thought was for the stock. Henschel must have forgotten to lock up the night before. Takings were down on the month. When the pressure was on, the ex-fighter tended to hit the bottle.

Duncan went in stealthily. Henschel was leaning on the bar waiting for him, unshaven, chin nestling in the neck of a yellowed sweater. He took one long look at Duncan and pushed some bills along the counter.

"There's two weeks pay there instead of notice. You're fired. And if them pricks weren't coming back, you and me'd have a bit of action."

Duncan stayed where he was. He looked unsuccessfully for his employer's glass. Henschel's small eyes were bloodshot but sober.

Duncan's voice was bewildered. "If *who* weren't coming back?"

Henschel spat violently into the cleaning-woman's bucket. "Don't give me that old toffee! Didn't I say it when I took you on—no law not under any circumstances! And what happens—I wind up with the bastards getting me out of my bed." He glowered at the entrance.

Duncan followed the baleful glare. Two men were coming down the arcade. The taller had been in the bar the night before. He was dressed as he'd been then--black Homburg and raglan-styled raincoat. He nodded at Henschel, lifting his arm in salute. His right thumb was missing. His partner was solidly square and younger with bright blond hair and flannel trousers that were too wide. He had a tough look and the hard assessing glance of the hunter. He turned it directly on Duncan.

"This him?"

Henschel spat into the bucket again and put the grille over the bottles on the shelves. He locked it ostentatiously and ducked under the counter.

"This is a bar—not the nick. How long you going to be here —he's fired, anyway."

The blond cop's voice was dubious. "No longer than necessary, Mr. Henschel. We appreciate this, really appreciate it."

Henschel slopped across the room in dirty sneakers. He stopped as he passed Duncan. "Mug!" he said heavily and turned to the young cop. "I'm going out to have some breakfast. Get him out of here before I come back." He slammed the doors hard behind him.

The blond perched himself on a stool and flashed a warrant card. He spoke confidently.

62

"Where are you living, Ritchie?"

The man in the black hat pulled out a notebook. Duncan walked across and lifted a chair down from a table.

"A hundred-and-twenty Tierney Street, Putney. And the name is Duncan."

"How long have you lived there?"

"Ten weeks."

"What time did you leave here last night?"

Duncan propped his head in his hands and looked at each man in turn.

"Henschel must have told you that already. I'm working the split-shift this week. I left here about nine-thirty. Why?"

The blond's smile seemed pasted on his face. "We're just making sure you're getting enough sleep, Ritchie. No other reason at all."

The man in the Homburg snapped his notebook shut. "Where's the package Linda Swann gave you?"

Duncan moved deliberately, putting the bar between them. He lowered the flap, feeling as if he'd been here before. This was definitely the cut-and-thrust of the Detectives Room. The fact that it made no sense didn't help him.

"Look," he offered. "You guys have already cost me my job. Why don't we settle for that? You look for another suspect—I look for another job. Who in hell is Linda Swann?"

The older man shook his head. "You were talking to her when I came in last night. She passed something over the bar to you—where is it?"

Duncan fished a cigarette from his pocket. The envelope he touched was suddenly very heavy. He imagined this pair shaking the contents out on the table—heartily amused as they saw the jewels torn from their settings—or whatever that tramp had stolen. She'd been scared, all right. The guy in the Homburg must have tailed her into the bar. He tried desperately to recall the man who'd gone to the table with her. Not that it mattered—these people wouldn't believe anything he said.

Somehow he managed a look of understanding. "Christ,

that! I'll get it for you." He was in the stockroom before they could prevent him. He worked fast, opening the door onto the alley and shoving the folded envelope under the base of the nearest garbage can. He shut the door again without sound and tiptoed across the room. The shelf was crowded with objects that had been left in the bar. He grabbed a forgotten paperback and went back to the waiting men. He laid it on the counter and said nothing.

The blond vaulted the bar, kicked up the flap and jerked his head at it.

"Get out there," he ordered savagely.

Duncan went through. The man with the Homburg swung his maimed hand catching the Canadian across the mouth. Duncan staggered, feeling the blood well from his cut lip.

"Empty your pockets," the detective said. Duncan made a pile of the few things he was carrying. Cigarettes, lighter, the money Henschel had just paid him. "Straddle!" said the cop. Duncan stood with his legs wide apart. The man ran expert fingers over his body. The blond came from the stock-room, wiping dust and dirt from his clothes and hands. "Nothing," he said openly. He picked up the paperback novel and sent it skimming across the room. Then he came round the bar and took a long hard look at Duncan.

"You've got a record, mister. Nobody owes you any favours. But you're being used. She's made a fool of a lot of people. You can't afford it. All we want is that package. You can stand on me — there'll be no charge."

Duncan put his things back in his pocket. The door to the alleyway hadn't been opened — he was certain of it.

"I don't know what you're talking about," he said evenly. "The book's what she handed over the bar. And that's the best I can do for you."

The blond nodded. "All right, Ritchie. Have it your own way. Now get the hell out of it!"

Duncan picked his sweater off the floor. His mouth was still bleeding. He held his handkerchief to it and walked out into the arcade. An orange sun hung behind a misty veil. The air was both damp and cold. He started down the hill, looking for the police-car that had to be there. The only parked vehicles were unloading merchandise. But any one of them might be a Q-van—plastered with innocuous advertising and carrying two-way radio and a powerful motor. This green delivery wagon, for instance. He made himself saunter as he neared it. The driver was deep in the list of runners at Sandown Park.

He walked on, wondering when the cops would make their move. They hadn't arrested him because they were waiting for him to lead them somewhere—but *where*, back to his room? They'd already established where he lived. They might even be waiting there now. Waiting for him to be present at a search for whatever they had planted there. The blond would have just the right manner for a magistrate's court.

"The articles produced in evidence were found at the lodgings of the defendant, sir. He refused to say how they came to be in his possession."

Much of what they'd said back in the bar made only too good sense. The girl had known she was being followed. They'd have had their own reasons for not pinching her the night before. But once she *was* in the lock-up she had broken her neck to get him in there with her. He couldn't be sure that she wouldn't have known he had a record. In fact, he could be sure of nothing. The first thing to do was get rid of whoever they'd put on his tail.

He hauled himself onto the northbound bus and sat close to the platform. Two people boarded the bus with him. An elderly woman with a string shopping bag, a red-faced man wearing a stiff white collar and elastic-sided boots. He unfolded a newspaper and started filling in a word-square. Duncan tendered a three-stage fare and kept his eyes on the traffic-signals coming up. The bus stopped on the crown of the highway. He stiffened in readiness. As green replaced red he leaped for the platform and swung himself into the air. He clung to the rail with one hand, legs pumping as they hit the ground. He released his hold, running in a confusion of wild horns, swerving cars and screams. The bus was fifty yards away, travelling at top speed. The redfaced man on the platform was ringing the bell furiously.

Duncan trotted back towards the bridge. A stitch bothered him high in the ribs. The woman who'd screamed looked after him, her hand to her mouth. No one else bothered. He ran down the steps leading to the river's edge. It was quiet there, a world completely apart. A cat lay among the reeds, ears flattened, tail waving, watching the gulls that swooped low over the dirty-brown water. The only person in sight was a small boy dredging with a holed pail. Duncan followed the muddied path downstream. His first stunned groping for understanding was over. The implications of his position needed no more thought. The girl would continue to say she'd given him whatever it was that she'd stolen. And the law would insist that he was in on the deal. She'd been in the *Cintra* enough times for Henschel to remember. If he didn't, that redheaded bastard would. The police could maintain that she went into the bar to establish contact and get instructions. With his record, anything was possible. They knew that finally he'd have to return to his room. He was a dead duck without clothes, passport and money. But before anything he had to retrieve the envelope and for that he needed darkness.

It was after five when he climbed the steps under a low cloudless sky. Putney High Street was thronged with people on their way home. He avoided the lights, hiding his face as he walked a few yards into the arcade. A couple of men were sitting up at the bar talking to Henschel. Cops or not, they weren't regulars. He left the arcade and walked a block south, circling into the alleyway. There were no street-lamps. The only light came from the rear of the business premises on the hill. He ducked into a doorway as a man shouted goodnight. Seconds later a motor-cycle stuttered past, its headlamps throwing an erratic shaft that just missed him. He ran to the back door of the *Cintra*. Bottles clinked as he lifted the garbage can. His fingers closed on the square of paper. A hundred yards away, he examined it in the flare of a match. The roll of film in the container made no sense. He had a peculiar feeling of uneasiness.—A film pack didn't warrant all this action. He slipped it back in its container and hurried down the hill. The CLOSED sign was up on all but one counter in the post office. He bought a registered envelope and addressed it with his left hand, in straggling block characters.

RITCHIE DUNCAN
C/O CANADA HOUSE
COCKSPUR STREET
W.1.

He dropped the film inside and handed it to the clerk. The receipt for the registered package he mailed to himself in care of a travel agency. Impulse sent him to the trash-basket. He picked up the film's original wrapping, straightened out the creased folds. A return address was printed on the back of the envelope. FARADAY ELECTRONIC RESEARCH. He shredded the paper into small pieces and committed the name to memory.

The hill was still crowded. He passed the store-Santa in a red hood and cotton whiskers, the eager-eyed kids milling round the sack of gifts, the small circle of Salvationists beating a drum outside the corner pub. *Make it on home, chum,* he told himself. *Like all the other good people. Cops may be waiting but make it on home!* He buttoned his shirt to the neck, suddenly cold. Not a door in the city he could knock on and ask for help. Martin Pole . . . Martin would have him in the house just about long enough to make a transatlantic call. And naturally Flora would speak for the family—he could hear her high, clear voice.

"My God, no! Not again." There'd be the pause to establish regret before rejection, then "No, Martin—it's just hopeless. There's nothing that anyone can do for Ritchie now. Just spend whatever money is necessary to keep it out of the papers."

He dropped off the bus at the bottom of Tierney Street. He had about a hundred yards to walk. All the cars parked under the lamps looked familiar. The doctor's Jaguar. The beat-up jaloppy with its ribald painted signs that belonged to the New Zealand kids. And Plotkin's station-wagon outside one hundred-and-twenty. He started up the street. He'd gone fifty yards when a motor roared behind him. He grabbed the railings. A car was coming at him fast, headlamps blazing, its front wheels on the sidewalk. He hurled himself to the ground, rolling sideways into the gutter. His body finished up underneath the parked Jaguar. The M.G. swung back into the road, cannoning off the Jaguar's rear end. Then its rear lights vanished round the corner. Sound of the crash hung in the quiet street.

He picked himself up and ran for the steps fronting one hundred-and-twenty. He was turning his key in the lock when he heard the shrill summons of a police whistle, the shouts from the doctor's house. He shut the door and leant against it dizzily. The split-second before the headlamps blinded him had been enough to recognize the men in the front seat.

"Wot in the name of blazes is going on 'ere?" The caretaker wheezed from his own stairs into the hall. He shuffled forward, watery eyes staring at Duncan curiously.

A two inch strip of skin was missing from the Canadian's thumb. His mouth had started to bleed again but he felt nothing.

"Someone just sideswiped the doctor's car," he said shakily.

The caretaker sniffed. " 'e can afford it. Ten-and-six for a dose of jollop. I suppose you know you 'ad visitors?"

Duncan nodded. "Are they still here?"

The caretaker's teeth slipped with excitement. He anchored them with a dirty forefinger.

"Nah—they been gone hours. I wouldn't let the buggars in without a search-warrant. But they said they 'ad one. You're not in trouble again, mate, are you?"

Duncan laughed without knowing why. He pushed past and climbed the stairs painfully. The caretaker followed. The room was in chaos. Curtains had been ripped from their hangings, the gas-stove dismantled, the bed upturned. His suitcase was in the middle of the floor, the locks forced open. He lifted the lid. The small leather folder inside had been opened but the contents were intact. Birth-certificate, passport, money. The caretaker spoke from the doorway.

"I seen it all. I asked that Plotkin to come and watch but 'e said 'e didn't want to be mixed up in no trouble. You could sue 'em, you know! You got a case! I'll bear witness, mate. And if you want to 'ide anything, the boilerhouse is the place. They could search till they got corns on their 'ands like I got on me feet." His small eyes grew cunning.

Duncan righted the bed and sat on it. "Shut that door." The old man slopped over, his head cocked in anticipation. Duncan chose his words. "It's a long story. Those guys weren't cops, Jim. I've got to get out of here now—tonight. Can you get me out the back way?" He gave the man a couple of fivers.

The caretaker's arthritic fingers closed on the money. He pushed it deep in the recesses of his baggy trousers and drew a finger across his gullet.

"Through the boilerhouse—you come out on Maxwell Street. Them geezers were looking for something, Canada. You can tell me. I don't talk."

Duncan ran hot water into the wash-basin. The lie had to be lurid enough to satisfy senile delinquency. He named a name common in crime reports—an ex-con turned elder statesman of the underworld.

"Manny Garber sent them. He thinks I've got something that belongs to him. He's wrong."

The caretaker lingered long on the name. "Manny Garber —'e's the guvnor in the West End, ain't 'e?"

Duncan wiped his face and hands. A strip of plaster covered his thumb, a patch his cut lip. He drew a chink in the curtains. The doctor's street door was wide open. A knot of people clustered round the damaged Jaguar. A uniformed constable was walking about, notebook open.

"Go downstairs and unbolt the back door," he said, "but don't go out on the street. I'll be down in a minute."

He put on a clean shirt and changed into his good suit

and overcoat. He packed everything he owned into the damaged suitcase. The locks still held. He left the house-keys on the table and cut the lights. He stood on the landing for a moment, watching as the door across the way opened fractionally. An eye peered out —a chestnut swimming in glycerine. A smell of haddock came from behind it.

"If you've got anything dodgy, Plotkin, get rid of it," Duncan said in a stage whisper. "They're on to us."

The door closed hurriedly. He tiptoed down the stairs, carrying his suitcase. The caretaker was waiting in front of the old-fashioned oil-burner. He pitched his voice above the bubbling in the rows of lagged pipes.

"It's unlocked—all you got to do is push."

Duncan gave him his hand. "I'll see you, Jim. And thanks."

The caretaker nodded. "Good luck, mate. And stand on me—if them bleeders come round 'ere agin, I'll put a flea in their ears, Manny Garber or no Manny Garber."

Duncan opened the door cautiously. He was at the bottom of a well with railings overhead. Steps led up to street level. He heard the bolts fastened on the inside of the back door. A woman's heels rattled by on the opposite pavement. Other than for her, the street was empty. He picked up his bag and hurried after her.

Hugh Morgan

HE was crossing the small vestibule when the telephone in his living-room started to ring. It was as if the caller had gauged his return to the second. He opened his door hurried-ly and lifted the receiver. The code greeting was superfluous, the familiar voice quietly authoritative.

"We're hoping to see you later, Hugh. Say about seven-thirty. Sandwiches and beer with some chess afterwards. Till later, then."

He put the phone down thoughtfully. The journey to

Dulwich would take him best part of an-hour-and-a-half. His day had been normal enough. The call they had promised to make about Linda had come through soon after his arrival at the office. He had relayed the news of her absence to Personnel. They'd been incurious, supplying him with a girl from the pool to handle the meagre correspondence. As far as he knew, there had been no query from Security. The nonsense had started only after he left Faraday's. Someone had followed him. The farcical mixture of threat and cajolery they were treating him to was absurd. While they skipped about behind lamp-posts, he was risking his liberty. People like Ashe and now this doctor used their authority without any imagination at all.

No one had given him the smallest sign of recognition from the beginning—just criticism and now suspicion.

He left his Faraday pass on the table and looked round the flat, checking the back door and windows. It was dry outside and colder. He exchanged his mac for a warmer coat, walked as far as the library and took a bus to the subway. He waited for a northbound train and stood inside the coach near the exit. The ferrule of his umbrella prevented the rubber-edged doors from closing. They rolled back to free themselves from the obstruction. He used the fraction of a second to step back onto the track. The train pulled out. He changed tracks and boarded a southbound train surfacing at Victoria. The blustering wind across the forecourt of the station sent pedestrians scurrying for shelter. He climbed to the upper deck of an empty bus, satisfied that he had shaken-off whoever might still have been following him. He left the bus at Dulwich and started up the long slope down which they'd taken him last night. Tried and tested, without a towel pulled over his head—bloody fools. He was halfway up the rise when a motor-cycle passed him. He thought he recognized Ashe underneath the helmet and goggles. He turned through the open gates. The brass plate was readable in the light thrown by the street-lamp.

COLIN FREW M.D. D.DC. DIPL. PSYCHOL.

There was no reference to surgery hours. The driveway was gloomy with unkempt laurel bushes. From the edge of the croquet lawn the house itself looked dead. But a dog started to bark long before he unfastened the gates to the stableyard. The motorcycle was propped against the wall, the crash-helmet dangling from the handlebars. A door opened across the yard. The blond driver looked out. He beckoned, seeing Morgan. A slit of light touched the blond's face. It was oddly enquiring—as if the man expected a whispered confidence. The room upstairs was sealed by overlapping curtains. The fire burned brightly. Morgan nodded to each person in turn. They were all there. The doctor and his woman, Ashe, the masseur and the thumbless man who'd been in the bar and of course the blond. They were grouped around the table with the exception of Ashe who was standing. Frew's head was down. He was aimlessly marking paper with pencil.

Ashe's metallic voice broke the silence. "I have some bad news for you. Whoever has the film it's certainly not Miss Swann."

Morgan half-rose from his chair, shocked and disbelieving. "That's ridiculous. I don't *make* mistakes like that." He looked at the watchful faces, seeking reassurance.

Ashe waited till Morgan sank back in the armchair. "There's a barman in the *Cintra*—a Canadian—do you know him?"

The recollection was clear. A tall man with a civil manner. They had talked music one evening while he'd waited for Linda.

"I've seen him half-a-dozen times. Why?"

Ashe frowned. "But you know who I mean. We don't think the film was ever left in the girl's house. We think she took it to the bar and gave it to this man before you arrived. I must know why. What do you think?"

Morgan's gesture was definite. She was incapable of deceiving him. He knew every banal thought in her head. "I think it's fantastic. I've been going in this bar with her on and off for months. She's never even spoken to the barman—why should she?"

Ashe's face was even redder than usual from the heat of the fire. He wiped it with a spotted handkerchief.

"That's what I intend to find out. She's upstairs. See what you can do with her."

Morgan got to his feet. "How long has she been here?"

Ashe looked at him steadily. "Since twenty to eight this morning. She had no chance to hide anything. She certainly wasn't on her way to you with the film."

The doctor stopped his scribbling and raised his head. His voice was soft.

"You'll find her sleepy, I expect, but she's quite capable of making sense."

The key was in the door facing the head of the stairs. Morgan turned it on a pleasant room with a green carpet and gilt furniture. The warm air was heady with freesias. A heater glowed at the foot of the bed. Linda was lying curled in foetal position, an eiderdown spread across her shoulders. He had to say her name twice before she heard him. She struggled up, looking at him with red swollen eyes. He held her tight till she had ceased to shake, stroking her hair mechanically.

"Where's the film, Linda?" He asked quietly. "You must tell me."

She touched his face with cold fingers. "Don't leave me, Hugh," she whispered. "I'm frightened."

He took her cheeks in his hands and turned her head. "They wouldn't let me see you before. I've been here since yesterday. I promise I won't leave you. But you must tell me what you've done with the film, Linda."

Her eyelids flickered. "The man in the bar—the Canadian."

He rocked her head gently. "The truth, Linda—it's our only chance. They'll kill us otherwise."

She nodded vaguely. "There was a man—man with a thumb missing—he followed me from the house, I was frightened."

He held her still tighter. "But you told me it was still in the house—*why?*"

She sat up, looking round the room as if fearful of being overheard. The words were only just audible.

"They're putting things in my food—drugs."

Her face was flushed and her eyes heavy but no more so than sleep would account for. He patted her shoulder.

"You're imagining things."

She shook her head. "No. It muddled me at first. Then came this glow and I began to feel *part* of things. I could see through walls. What really terrifies me is that it all makes sense. You realize that man's a doctor, do you?" She peered into his face anxiously.

"That's lunacy," he said abruptly. He took his hands away suddenly loathe to touch her.

Her eyes became sly. "He tries to get inside my brain to know what I'm thinking. But I've kept him out, Hugh. He doesn't know about the barman."

"*Listen* to me," he burst out. "There's no doctor and no drugs. These men want the film. Unless you tell me what happened to it, we'll never get out of here alive. Do you understand that?"

Her mouth crumpled with effort. "Yes."

He went on urgently. "We'll be married and go away somewhere—South Africa or New Zealand. I'll take care of you—we'll forget about all this. But first you must think. You gave the film to the Canadian because you were frightened. Then what happened?"

She spoke, staring into space. "It was in an envelope. He put it in his pocket. When I went back he was gone."

"He might have left it behind," he suggested. "Did you ask when you went back?"

She shook her head obstinately. "He wouldn't. He wouldn't give it to anyone but me. I know that."

"And then you went to his house, is that it?" he urged.

She turned a bewildered look on him. "How could I—nobody knew where he lived."

Her eyes were guileless but they'd been guileless before

74

and twice she had lied. Truth seemed to be irrelevant to her. He struck her across the face deliberately. The words came easily, the pent-up hatred of the past months.

"You stupid neurotic bitch—useless in bed and out of it! You're going to die and you're determined to take me with you."

She grabbed him by the jacket. "It's not true—Hugh—look at me!"

He picked off her hand with distaste. "Don't you think I've had *enough* of looking at you?"

Her mouth framed words that never came. Then she started to laugh, rocking to and fro, the tears spilling down her cheeks.

He stepped outside quickly and turned the key on her hysteria. They were waiting for him down below. He faced them nervously.

"I was wrong. She did give it to the Canadian."

Ashe shifted a pile of books and flipped a switch. A motor whirred high on the shelf. A tape started to turn on a recording-machine. There was the sound of the door being opened and shut—the creak of bed-springs—Morgan's voice. *"Where's the film, Linda? you must tell me."* The tape ended on her high-pitched laughter. Ashe stopped the machine, looking at Frew questioningly.

The doctor buttered bread and spread it with Stilton. He wiped his fingers on a napkin and refolded it neatly.

"I'm not convinced. The real answer may well lie in the no-man's-land between truth and falsehood. We'll have to see."

Ashe nodded. "I agree. But we can't waste time. As far as you're concerned, Morgan, the whole thing's a closed book. Put it out of your mind. You're going to have to deal with more important matters. Someone's arriving from Belgium tomorrow. Someone who wants to see you."

Everybody turned towards him. The blond threw him a vague gesture of congratulation. Even the masseur was smiling. He found himself smiling in return. He lit a cigarette, speaking to Frew with newfound ease.

"Her mind's unbalanced, of course. You heard that bit about the drugs?"

Frew hid his nose in his hand for a moment. "She's had sedatives," he said at last. "She's an obvious schizophrenic. The first clinical examination she has will establish the fact. Then she'll be committed to an asylum."

Morgan reached for an ash-tray. They were still looking at him. He had the impression he was meant to comment.

"Won't she talk?" he asked casually. "I thought it was decided that she knew too much?"

Frew smiled brilliantly. "That was before we realized that she might be a more important catch than we imagined. Certainly she'll talk but asylum staffs are used to auditory delusions. What we want to know we'll find out. Don't worry about it."

Ashe looked at his watch. "That's right—get it out of your mind. We'll be in touch some time tomorrow. I'll see that someone makes the proper noises about Swann's absence—I mean at Faraday's. You just go on the way you usually do. Goodnight."

Morgan gave each one his hand. The blond let him out of the house. He left the train at Putney Station, sure this time that he was not being followed. He took the short way home, the towpath behind the brewery. Giant stacks erupted into the night, the glow reflected in the waste of water. The wind whipped through the patch of willows ahead. He started to walk a little more quickly. He was deep into the shadows when the figure ran from behind a tree. An arm rose and fell. Morgan took five stumbling steps before his head split with pain. The arm rose and fell again. The last blow sent Morgan face down into the swiftly-running water.

Ritchie Duncan

THE hotel corridor was narrow and gloomy with windows overlooking the railroad tracks. The panes had been painted on the outside. A much-fingered card was looped over the handle to the elevator gates.

LIFT TEMPORARILY OUT OF ORDER
PLEASE USE STAIRS

The lobby had a French Line poster, two pot-plants and a collection of out-of-date airline schedules. The woman behind the desk took the pencil out of her mouth. She had smudged eyes and made quick nervous gestures as if her hands were unaccustomed to repose. She smiled at Duncan.

"Good-morning, sir. Are you staying on tonight or not?"

He left his room-key on the desk. The place was a dump. Bells went unanswered. The whole building shook with the arrival or departure of each train. But the rates were low.

"For a couple of days, I guess."

She pencilled something on the floor-plan in front of her. "Anything you need, if you'll tell the maid," she said mechanically.

He gave her the nod of belief she expected and pushed the revolving door. The street outside was standard for an approach to any mainline railroad terminal. Phoney Lost Property Offices offered canvas luggage, simulated suede coats and transistor radios. Garish windows displayed diamond-chip engagement rings and Birmingham trinkets. Queers, cheap whores and transient hoodlums patronized the all-night coffee bars. There were half-a-dozen pubs, a striptease cellar with pictures of over-developed busts outside, the inevitable Madame Sylvie hawking French lessons and "specialized services."

businesses had a look of seedy impermanence as if their owners accepted the imminent arrival of the bulldozers. It was a street of false names and fugitive identities. A questionable place to hide even if you knew what you were hiding from.

Duncan left the subway at Trafalgar Square, turning up the collar of his overcoat. The day was grey with damp fingers that tweaked at joints and muscles. He climbed steps in a block that was almost entirely Canadian. Banks, government buildings, shipping companies, insurance. A stringy-haired brunette with a Nova Scotian whine produced the registered envelope, compared the address with the details in Duncan's passport and gave him a book to sign.

He undid the envelope as he walked up the Strand heading for a camera store that advertised rapid development. He left the film for processing, giving the name he was using at the hotel. He called Tierney Street from a booth in the post-office at St. Martin's Lane. The caretaker's voice was wheezy and petulant.

"You'll 'ave to speak up, 'ooever it is. I can't 'ear a word."

Duncan spoke close to the mouthpiece. "It's Ritchie. What's happening?"

The caretaker affected a sort of obsequious whine. "Good-morning, Mr. Belton. No sir, the plumbers ain't been near. One moment, sir. There's too much noise going on." A door was shut firmly. The old man's voice lapsed to normal. "That was that Plotkin—standing on the stairs earwigging. They been back twice, last night and this morning—asking for your address—'oo yer frens were and all that. I seen Plotkin chatting them up. The blond one give me a fiver. If you phoned, I 'ad to tell you some girl 'ad been 'ere asking for you. Girl name of Swann. 'e give me a number where you was supposed to ring 'er. Flaxman 9872."

Duncan tucked the receiver under his chin while he scribbled the number on a scrap of paper.

"Thanks, Jim. Now listen—I'm getting out of the country tonight. As soon as I hit lucky, I'll send you a few quid —ok?"

He had a strong urge to end the conversation there. You

didn't have to be a cop to get the equipment for line-tapping. He relaxed. They might be able to tap the line but only the Law could trace the source of a call.

"Gotcher, mate," the old man answered. "I ain't doing this for money though. 'ere—I 'ad a go at them about not being coppers."

Duncan stiffened. "And?"

The caretaker snickered. "It was a right giggle. 'im with the black 'at says 'you want to put it to the test?' I said they'd be 'earing from my legal advisers. Plotkin says they're from the Special Branch but 'e knows it all, don't 'e?"

Duncan hung up and dialled Directory Enquiries. The operator refused to supply an address for the number the caretaker had given him. He spun the dial again. FLA 9872. The line clicked open but nobody spoke. He heard the sound of guarded breathing. He faked a Germanic accent, altering the final digit.

"Please—this is Flaxman 9873?"

The line went dead. He left the booth wiping hands that had suddenly become sticky. He turned into the public library at the top of Panton Street. A girl supplied him with an armful of reference books. He carried them to a quiet corner and started to check out the Faraday Electronic Research Company. A fifteen-minute search provided certain basic information. A list of the firm's directors, the date of the company's formation and its purpose. The name Faraday appeared in two trade journals over conservatively-worded advertisements. He read through the Voters List for the Hampton Court area. Only four names were given for the Faraday address. He pushed back his chair. He couldn't even be certain that she worked at Faraday's. She could have picked up the envelope anywhere. This Flaxman number was obviously bait. He turned in his books and cut across the square back to the camera store. The salesman took his slip and walked over to a tray of finished work. He came back carrying an orange folder and a can of film. He touched a bell and smiled.

79

"I think our dark-room manager wants a word with you, sir."

Duncan pushed the film and folder into his pocket and put some money on the counter.

"I don't have time—I'm in a hurry."

A white-coated man with rimless spectacles was already coming through from the back room.

"Mr. Rawlings?" he asked.

Duncan hesitated. The exit to the street showed none of the lurking figures he expected. The dark-room manager's face was no more than mildly curious.

"Yes," said Duncan.

The man shook his head. "Do you realize you only used eight frames out of thirty-six? We can cut film for you any length you like, sir. Incidentally, the quality of your work is excellent. I've seldom had sharper negatives brought in. Most interesting. I'd say a Cannon, F4 at about a 250th—am I right?"

It was obvious that his interest was entirely professional. Duncan smiled.

"I wouldn't know. I didn't take the pictures. But I'll pass on the good word."

He walked as far as the Trafalgar Square fountain and opened the folder. There were eight prints. Each portrayed a document. The print and symbols were too small to be deciphered without an enlarger. But the headlines were clearly legible.

Project A. Lederle TOP SECRET CLASSIFIED.

He stuffed the pictures back in his pocket hastily and looked round. The square was an oasis in a desert of noise. Nelson stared sternly at the skyline, high on his plinth. Stone lions lurked below. A mistress herded a crocodile of flat-hatted schoolgirls up the steps to the National Gallery. Tourists posed for a bottlenosed photographer, pigeons fluttering on their heads and arms. Trafalgar Square at eleven in the morning. About as sinister as a gathering of the Society of Friends.

The rest was supposed to be simple. All he had to do was

get to Scotland Yard as fast as he could and tell his tale. The moment he arrived the phone would already be ringing down in the Criminal Records office. His own record would precede him up to the Assistant-Commissioners Department. There'd be a long wait while cops made unnecessary journeys to get a good look at him. Finally, Authority with a military manner and sceptical eyes would listen as Duncan talked.

"I was working in the *Cintra* in Putney. A couple of days ago a girl I knew by sight came in. She left an envelope behind the bar. A couple of phoney cops tried to get it back. The same night they aimed a black M.G. at me. I beat them by a tenth of a second."

The faint smile was easy to imagine. "And where is this envelope?"

He pushed the folder deep in his overcoat pocket. The pieces of the puzzle were moving like metal scraps attracted to a magnetic base. Whatever Project A. Lederle was, it was certain that he was walking around with confidential information that the girl had stolen. She wouldn't be working alone. Whether or not she was employed at Faraday's, she'd need help. Who likelier than the guy she visited the bar with—the one she'd met that night—the shabby character who had hurried her out. The answer was that they were in this caper together, selling Faraday secrets to a competitor. Why people would be ready to kill because of the secrets was something again.

One thing was sure. With his record, it didn't matter whether a strip of film or a handful of jewellery was involved. The Director of Public Prosecutions office would work out a formula that would convict him. He pitched his butt into the fountain. There was one law all these people were forgetting. In order to lose, you had to have a chance to win.

He flagged a cab and drove back to the Paddington hotel. He kept it waiting long enough to leave his passport up in his room. He directed the driver to Victoria station and paid him off. He deposited the film and prints in a coin-operated storage-box at the end of the Continental Departure tracks. Then he walked to the Imperial War Museum. He wasted a half-hour circulating among the relics of forgotten campaigns. Captured regimental colours drooped over muzzle-loading cannons, the legends part of military history. Wellington — Ashanti — Khartoum — Kitchener. He hung around near a display of tribal weapons till that corner of the gallery was clear. The nearest footsteps were rooms away. He climbed over the rope barrier and lifted a sheaf of iron-barbed arrows from a hide sheath. The storage-box key dropped out of sight in the quiver. He replaced the arrows and wiped the dust from his fingers. The key was as safe there as in a bank vault.

It was nearly two when he arrived at Hampton Court. A boy directed him to Faraday's — over the bridge and along the path by the river. A red-brick wall enclosed what looked like extensive grounds. Winter had trimmed the grass and undergrowth on the bank between the path and the wall. It was almost pastoral with willows bowed over the river, duck cruising in the reeds, the absence of noise. The towpath was deserted. He hurled himself into a tree and wedged his feet in the branches. They swayed under his weight. He could see over the top of the wall. The house was a hundred yards away — an E-shaped mansion with its wings facing the river. A glass-topped tower rose above a compound surrounded by barbed wire. Inside was an acre or so of flat-roofed buildings glistening with moisture. There were no windows.

He lowered himself to the ground. Another quarter-mile and he climbed a fence into a quiet road lined with trees. The front entrance to Faraday's was guarded by two lodges. Solid gates blocked the driveway. He strolled by, propped himself against a tree and waited. It was ten minutes before anyone appeared — a middle-aged man with the gait of one whose eye is on the clock. Duncan stepped from behind the tree.

"Excuse me — do you know Miss Swann?"

The man was obviously harassed by the exigencies of courtesy.

"Swann? Let me see now, I certainly know the name . . . wait a minute . . . that's right—she was in Records with Hugh Morgan."

Duncan fell into step beside him. "You say 'was'—doesn't she work here any more?"

The man looked at him oddly. "I think you'd better ask in there." He hurried into the gate-lodge.

Duncan gave him a couple of minutes then followed. His feet clattered over bare boards. A counter ran the length of the room. A flap at the end gave access to an inner door on to the driveway. Time-clocks hung on the wall with racks of cards under them. A man in battledress and a beret was leaning on the counter watching Duncan carefully.

"I'm trying to locate a Miss Swann," the Canadian smiled.

The guard shifted his stance. "Then you picked the wrong day. She's not in."

Duncan folded a pound-note and put it on the counter. "I've lost her address."

The guard left the money where it lay. "That's what they all say. Is she a friend of yours?"

Duncan juggled his shoulders. "Well *you* know—not exactly a friend. Somebody suggested I should look her up but if she's not here . . ." He put the bill back in his pocket, turning when he was halfway to the door. "How about Hugh Morgan—is he in?"

The name produced the same odd reaction. The guard studied him for fully three seconds. "What did you say your name was?" he asked.

"Rawlings."

The guard picked up a phone, cupping his hand over the mouthpiece. His voice was too low to hear more than an occasional word. He cradled the receiver and composed his face to a stiff smile.

"Would you like to come this way, Mr. Rawlings?"

He accompanied Duncan through the inner door on to a tarmac driveway. He pointed to a man dressed in similar uniform waiting outside the Security tower. "He'll take care of you."

Duncan mounted the stairs and opened the door at the top. The room had one enormous window giving a clear view of most of the house and grounds. There were French prints on the walls, a minimum of office furniture and three coloured phones on a gate-legged table. The man sitting behind it wore a dark suit and black tie. His bald brown head had the polish of a horse-chestnut. He had a fleshy nose and active eyes. He terminated their inspection of Duncan with an abrupt question.

"Precisely what is your business here, Mr. Rawlings?"

The Canadian sat where he was expected to sit, with the light full on his face.

"I'm enquiring after Miss Swann."

"I gathered that much." The man flicked the question across the room. "Why?"

Duncan took it on the bounce. "Why what? Incidentally, I didn't get your name."

The man's hands made a gesture of enclosure. "Major Sangster. I'm in charge of security here."

Duncan shrugged. "I see. Well in that case I don't think you'll be very interested in me, Major. All I wanted was a word with Miss Swann."

There was a file on the table near Sangster. He opened it at random, his fingers playing with the edges of the pages.

"Have you got any identification with you, Mr. Rawlings?" he asked suddenly. "A driving-licence or something of the sort." He extended a hand in readiness.

"No," said Duncan. He looked at the other long enough to make his point. "The only time I get asked for a passport is coming into the country."

Sangster's face reddened a little. "If you're concerned about my right to ask that sort of question, Mr. Rawlings, let me say this. You happen to be on protected premises. Rest assured that this gives me adequate authority."

A dynamo outside settled into a high whine that punished Duncan's ear-drums. He had a strong impression that in some way he was being tested—that Sangster was bluffing. He eased himself lower in his chair and stretched his legs as far as they would go.

"That's all very interesting but there's one thing we'd better get straightened out, Major Sangster. There's a sign outside your gates that says ENQUIRIES. That presupposes people who'll be asking questions. I'm on your protected premises only because you invited me. Now I'm proposing to walk right on out of them. If I have to give a fuller explanation than that to anyone I guess we'll be able to handle the situation."

Sangster locked the file away in a steel cabinet. When he swung round his face was shrewd.

"You're a reporter, aren't you, Rawlings. I can smell you chaps a mile away. Well there's no story for you here. I left the coroner's court an hour ago. The verdict was 'Death by misadventure'. You can't get any news value out of Morgan now. It's too late. Would you like a drink before you leave?"

Duncan waved a hand. "And Miss Swann?"

Sangster had his head in a cupboard. He turned holding a glass of scotch to the light. He disposed of it, locked the cupboard again and sat down.

"What paper do you work for?"

Duncan was sure now of his ground. "I freelance. Wherever they buy I sell."

Sangster sighed heavily. "It's the truth. There's no story for you here. What happened has been coincidence all along the line. We suspected here that the girl's breakdown was imminent. There was a definite history of mental instability. Neither she nor Morgan had access to classified information —there's no drama. They both happened to be employed in what is no more really than a reference library. You probably know we're engaged in work of national importance. We don't want either notoriety or advertisement. Try to make something sensational out of any of this and you'll find that we know how to apply the gag."

Duncan came to his feet. Instinct told him Sangster knew nothing of the film.

"I'll kill this story where it started if things are the way you say they are. But I'm still going to check out the facts. Call it professional zeal if you like. You can save me shoe-leather. Where *is* the girl?"

Sangster pinched his nose before answering. He made his throwing-away gesture again—as if ridding himself of responsibility.

"Are you giving me your word, Rawlings?"

It cost an effort to keep the eagerness out of his voice. "Yes."

Sangster lowered his voice. "It's a sad business. A solicitor acting for the family phoned me this morning. The girl was admitted during the night for observation—hallucinations, threats of suicide—the lot. The asylum is somewhere near Ascot—the Brierley Mental Nursing Home—that's all I know."

Duncan considered first one foot then the other. "You've been frank with me, Major. Strictly off the record, I hear there was something more between Morgan and the girl than just a working relationship."

Sangster smiled with a hint of caution. "My secretary happens to be over at the house at the moment but she's twenty-two, unmarried and developed in all the right places. Are you suggesting that we sleep together?"

Duncan's expression was bland. "You're not dead nor is she in a nursing-home."

Sangster pulled at his ear thoughtfully. "There are a hundred and seventeen people working on these premises. Clerks, chemists, typists, technicians and twenty of my own chaps. Part of my job is to know what they're all up to. I can tell you you're on the wrong track, Rawlings. Where did all this start, anyway. You keep saying 'I hear'—*where* do you hear?"

Duncan collected his overcoat. "You're far too intelligent to expect an answer to that one, Major. We'll settle for 'coincidence'—it seems to be a popular word at the moment. Well I'll be on my way. Once again, thanks for being so frank. It's appreciated."

Sangster shook hands as if too long a grip might betray a secret.

"Nice to have met you, Rawlings. Whenever there *is* a story worth telling at Faraday's you'll find we're as anxious to help you chaps as the next." He lifted a green telephone. Seconds later, a guard knocked on the door. Sangster spoke to him indifferently. "See this gentleman to the lodge, Gifford."

It was twenty-to-three when Duncan reached the bridge. He bought a newspaper and looked for somewhere to read it. There was a riverside café with a stucco front and false beams. He made his way in. The solitary waitress on duty rattled her litany with active displeasure.

"You're too late for the lunch; we only serve grills after two-thirty."

She flourished a greasy card under Duncan's nose. He took it gingerly. Liver-and-bacon. Eggs-and-bacon. Beans-on-toast.

"Eggs-and-bacon, please."

"One egg or two?" She made it plain that whichever way he opted it would be wrong. England, my England—where service had become construed with incivility. He managed to hold the comment back.

"Two please and fried on both sides."

She twisted the ring on her finger, admiring it from different angles.

"You want tea or coffee?"

"Water," he said and opened the newspaper. The report he was looking for was tucked away on the back page.

CORONER SAYS TOWPATH UNSAFE

An inquest was held today on Mr. Hugh Morgan late of 217 Ferndale Road, Putney. Mr. Morgan's corpse was recovered from the Thames last night by a River Police patrol. A Home Office pathologist giving evidence said that the body had been immersed in the water for about four hours. Death was due to drowning. Bruises at the base of the neck and on the skull were caused prior to death. Doctor Hector Verity, Coroner, said that there was no evidence to suggest that Morgan had met death other than by misadventure. An unconscious man's body might well drift into the path of moored craft and so occasion bruises. Deceased was locally employed and enjoyed the reputation of being an intelligent man with no worries. The accident had occurred along a stretch of towpath that was notoriously slippery after rain. There had been three such accidents in the area since he had taken office. Representations to the council to have railings erected had met with no success. The towpath was a short cut for people living in the Ferndale Road neighbourhood. It was used by children on their way home from school. He hoped the Press would give the widest publicity to his remarks. Mr. Morgan was thirty-five and left no next-of-kin.

He folded the newspaper and sat looking through the window at the water swirling below. Possession of the film seemed an invitation to disaster. Morgan drowned—the girl in an asylum. Sangster obviously wanted to block publicity but not because he knew the truth. Suppose you went to him and said, "I'm an ex-con just out of a job, not a reporter. Take a look at these prints—they might interest you."

There were half-a-dozen ways Sangster could play it but each involved the police. The best would be that they took Duncan's story at face-value. The worst was just as easy to imagine. Either way, they'd never feel sure that he hadn't retained copies of the film for some future use. The alternative was for him to go back to Tierney Street. put himself on show and wait for the other side to establish contact. And the moment he did that he'd be completely uninsurable.

What he needed was someone with authority, intelligence and a sense of justice. Finding such a person would be as easy as establishing Peter Pan's forwarding address. There *was* one logical thing for him to do—stay on the run. And his only help would come from those who knew what it was like to *be* on the run. Somebody like Chalice. Chalice slept late. There was small hope of getting in touch with him before night-time.

He stared disgustedly at the eggs skidding across his plate. He gave them best and asked for his bill. The waitress scratched her back hair with a pencil and spoke to him haughtily.

"Any complaints about your food?"

He laid some money on the table. "Yes. The eggs are about on a par with the service. Bad, just short of being offensive."

He rode the subway home and surfaced. A line of street-peddlers had trundled their push-carts to the corner, alert for passing cops. He bought a bag of fruit and carried it back into the subway entrance. He watched the entrance to the hotel till he was satisfied and then crossed the road. The woman in the lobby flashed him a mechanical smile.

"I'm going to try and get some sleep," he told her. "Give me a call about five."

The room was cold and cheerless, the windows rattling in their frames each time a train pulled in. He double-locked his door and tilted a chair under the handle. He lowered the venetian blinds and rolled himself in blankets. The phone startled him from a doze that had been made uneasy by half-glimpsed faces and whispering voices. He rolled over and answered the shrill summons. He bathed in a ringed and rusted tub to the melancholy sound of the plumbing overhead. Then he dressed and went downstairs.

Outside, coloured lights blinked invitation to cellar dives. Canned music jumped in a dozen doorways. The whores had already taken up their assault positions in the shadows. Duncan ducked down the hotel steps with head averted. The sooner he found another place to live the better. A neighbourhood like this was a magnet for a cop who was hard up for a pinch. It was no trick at all to make an arrest under the Suspected Persons Act. All the cop had to do was shut his eyes, spin round twice and grab.

He studied the map in the subway station. One change

took him to his destination. The ticket-collector at Islington directed him to Stacey Street. The Red Lion was a corner pub with two of its four bars half-full. He bought himself a drink and listened to the barmen's accents. A fat youngster with a strip of plaster over one eye looked the most likely. Duncan caught his attention.

"Does the name Harry Chalice mean anything to you?" he asked in a low voice.

The barman used the inside of his arm to wipe his forehead. "Is it beer you're after, Mister, or what?"

"Harry Chalice," Duncan repeated. "I was told I could get a message to him through you. How about it?"

The Irishman jerked three pints of beer, double-jumping the handle expertly to put a head on each glass.

"Were you now," he said in answer. "Well I've not seen him myself in six long weeks. Give me your name and I'll try to find out."

Duncan carried his drink to an empty table. A rat-haired brunette joined him almost immediately. The customers in the Red Lion seemed to obey a law of inversion. The shabbier the clothing, the more educated the accent. The actors and writers from the Canonbury settlement slouched in sweaters and sandals. Next to them, hard-eyed men in expensive clothing dropped aitches as if the loss were of no concern to them. The brunette sitting across the table lifted her glass, her voice moody.

"I suppose you're slumming, darling, are you?"

It was a Sloane Square voice with overtones of drama school. But a long time ago. She wore a black leather suit with a man's shirt. Her lipstick looked as if it had been applied without aid of a mirror.

Duncan glanced at her warily. She looked the kind of woman who would involve you in argument at the drop of a hat.

"Not exactly," he said. "I'm waiting for someone if that's all right with you." He smiled to take the edge off it.

She made a sweeping gesture of tolerance. "Anything's all right with me, darling. I'm the most liberal girl. Survey the scene while you're waiting. The famous and infamous. Islington is integrated. I suppose it's a man you're waiting for?"

He put his glass down carefully. "A man."

She sighed. "Me too, darling. But chin up—there are better days ahead."

She moved with sudden alacrity as a man in his early twenties approached the table. He had the build of a middleweight in training. Flat ears were pressed against a smallish head with good even features. He wore elegant hopsack and brilliant black brogues. He crossed his legs, scowling at the back of the woman now standing at the bar.

"You don't want to get lumbered with her. She's a right dragon. I'd like to fire her out of a cannon eleven hundred times only it wouldn't help. She'd bounce. Are you Ritchie Duncan?"

Duncan nodded. The man offered a well-manicured hand. "Crying Eddie. Harry sent me." He jerked his head at the door. He led the way outside, ignoring the acknowledgements from groups at the bar. A trio of string-tied youths were fumbling at the doorhandle of the parked E-type. He moved them on with his thumb, his voice sour.

"Why don't you nuts run on home—or don't you want to grow up and have troubles?" He waited till they'd disappeared round the corner and opened the car door for Duncan. "A couple of weeks in a remand home and they come round here acting like tearaways. No respect. They know this is Harry's car—it wouldn't stop them nicking it."

He gunned the motor, moving up through the gears with the practised skill of the expert driver. He handled the dark blue Jaguar with care and imagination until they were deep into Mayfair. He slid the car into a slot at the bottom of Queen Street and searched his pockets for a coin the right size.

"Parking meters," he said bitterly. "Them cops ought to be out catching burglars. Know what one of them said to me the other day. I said, "It's the Queen's Highway, ain't it?" 'Isn't it,' the bastard said," 'and you ain't got no right to park on it—just roll on it'." He sank a coin in the meter and locked the doors carefully. He signalled Duncan to follow him. It was colder but some of the dampness had gone from the air. They cut through Shepherd's Market and turned up Hertford Street, stopping at the top. A coaching lamp hung in a Regency fanlight. The black door was four-panelled. Gilt lettering on it proclaimed:

MANDRAKE'S MANOR   MEMBERS ONLY

Crying Eddie turned the handle. Nothing but wax had been used on the hall for two hundred years. He opened the door of what had originally been the drawing-room. Here only the ceiling was original. The lighting was pale green. A canopy extended over a bar built of black glass. Hungarian prints on the walls featured the discovery and despatch of Transylvanian werewolves. The table seats were small-scale models of electric chairs. An assortment of nooses, masks and instruments of torture were strewn about the place. In the middle of this, Chalice sat on his barstool looking like a cavalry commander contemplating a charge. Behind the bar was the blonde who had driven him to the prison, reading. Otherwise the room was empty.

Chalice slid to the floor, standing for a moment with legs apart, looking at Duncan. John Michael might have dressed him for the role. He wore charcoal grey slacks, handmade shoes with silver buckles, a cashmere sweater over an orange silk shirt. He came forward to envelop Duncan in a rough embrace.

"See, that!" he said to the girl delightedly. "My old cell mate out of C4/17! How's it going, Canada?"

The girl's fine fair hair was looped on top of her head and skewered with jewelled tortoiseshell. Bare shoulders rose from black velvet. She looked the age to be wearing an elder sister's clothes and obviously wasn't. She put her book down, winked at Duncan and returned to her reading.

Chalice's fingers found the grey streak in his hair. "Where'd you leave the car, Crying?" His manner was a mixture of authority and friendliness.

Crying Eddie shifted his morose stare from the girl behind the bar to Chalice. He chucked a set of ignition keys across the table.

"At the bottom of Queen Street. There'll be six of the bastards there by now waiting for the meter to run out."

Chalice put the keys away in a pocket. "Feed it on your way out. Are you going home now or round your bird's place?"

Crying Eddie flipped a coin, trapping it on the back of his hand. He peeped at the result reluctantly.

"Home. Suits me—I'll get into kip and watch telly. I'll just be in time to catch Inspector Lockhart. He kills me with that 'Let's go, Sergeant Baxter!'" He left the room making noises like a car being driven off at high speed.

Chalice nodded at the closing door. "Don't let Crying confuse you—he's a character. He's twenty-three years old and he's got more worries than you and me ever heard of. He worries about his health, the price of old gold, Terry Downes's hooter and whether his mother goes down his trousers while he's asleep. He's a natural worrier. He's worth twenty grand—never took a drink in his life and never done a day inside. He'd drive a car into a bank-vault and come out through the manager's office and he never stops moaning. Crying's my boy. He's proved it twenty times."

Duncan looked significantly at a corner table. "Could I have a word with you alone, Harry?"

Chalice went behind the bar and poured a couple of scotches. He reached out, taking the book from the girl's grasp.

"'Memoirs of a Lady-in-waiting' by Countess Ouspakaya! You must be joking, Kathy. Read it anyway. Me and my friend's talking business."

He brought the glasses over to the table and sat with his back to the bar. He let a notch out in his belt, his good-natured face suddenly serious.

"What's the trouble, old chum?"

Duncan hesitated. Back in the hotel bedroom everything had seemed much simpler. He lowered his voice.

"I'm on the run, Harry, as of yesterday. I need help."

Chalice produced a gold-edged wallet. He counted off twenty fivers and pushed them over the table.

"Ok," he said easily. "I'll fix you up with a drum to stay in while we have a go at straightening the law. If that's no good we'll have to get you another passport. Come to think of it, I'll row you in on the next bit of business I do. It'll give you a chance to earn." He clasped Duncan's fingers round the money on the table.

The Canadian shook his head. "It's not as simple as that. I don't even know what I'm on the run *from*."

Chalice made a gesture of resignation. "Do me a favour. Put that loot away before I stuff it in your earhole. See what happens—I spent best part of a year explaining the facts of life to you. You're out a couple of months and then back you go to your lark. It don't make sense, Ritchie."

Duncan pocketed the twenty bills. A grafter's generosity was the most uncomplicated in the world and entirely without strings. He was certain that acceptance of the hundred pounds committed him to nothing.

"Maybe it doesn't . . ." he started to admit.

Chalice broke in determinedly. "What do you get out of it, Ritchie? Creeping round some old bag's bedroom and hoisting jewellery she's got insured for twenty grand. *You* sell it to Nat The Eye for thirty-five hundred. Out of that your expenses have got to come. On top of that there's this lark you've got to know all about locks and keys. Now take me— all I need is one of Kathy's stockings and a pick-axe handle and I'm in business. And what I see, I take, Ritchie. *Money*."

Duncan wagged his finger. "If you'd shut up and listen you'd realize we're not talking about the same things. I can use this hundred quid but it's not what I came for. I need a different sort of help, Harry. I'm in the worst kind of trouble but not with the law."

Chalice knuckled his scalp. "What other kind is there?" he asked simply.

Duncan had a feeling of frustration. He'd shared a cell with Chalice long enough to know that the bewilderment was genuine. The guy was a direct throwback to the days of piratical free-for-alls. The same mentality—the same loyalties. Genial, shrewd and fiercely loyal to those he called his own, he was able to turn on commando ruthlessness at will. The headshrinkers, baffled by the simplicity of his philosophy, would identify him as a psychopath.

"Well," Duncan said finally. "Death's a sort of trouble if you want to go on living. A couple of guys did their best to run me down in a car last night. No accidents—they aimed. That's the story the short way—there's a lot more to it than that."

Chalice pushed his glass aside, the muscles by his eyes hardening.

"Do you know who they are—where they come from?"

Duncan lifted his shoulders. "No. I'll give this to you straight—Harry. I've gotten mixed up in something that's way beyond me."

Chalice swung round with the words. Before he could speak the girl had closed her book. She glanced at her watch resignedly.

"All right, Harry, I'll say it for you—'Why don't you take a walk, Kathy—as far as Liverpool and back for instance!'" She came round the end of the bar, swinging her hips in parody of a model's walk. A snow-leopard wrap trailed from her hand. She fluttered her fingers as she passed Duncan.

"Goodbye, dear. Nice to have met you."

Chalice smacked her rump. "Drop the latch as you go out. We can do without customers tonight. Me and my friend want to be alone." He waited till he heard the street door slam then went to the curtains. He watched her out of sight then touched the black drapes, shaking his head. They were decorated with cabalistic signs done in gold thread.

"Don't ask me," he said with a sort of wonder. "I don't understand none of it. She had some queer in from Chelsea —that bar alone cost six hundred quid. It's gone to 'er head. Know what she wanted to put on her passport application

—'Mayfair club-owner'. She's got twenty-six members—they've all done time. But to hear her at it, you'd think they was diplomats. It's a good way of losing steady money. Not that I mind, Ritchie. She gets a kick out of it and I've got more than enough coming in. Funny thing, I suppose I could turn the game up tomorrow and still have fifty on a horse when I fancied one."

"Then why don't you?" Duncan asked. "What's so clever about bucking the odds?"

Chalice turned on a record-player. The room was filled with the sound of Brubeck's sophisticated piano. "Some old bag lives upstairs," he explained, coming back to the table, his face pensive. "She bangs on the floor and listens at keyholes. Why don't I turn it up? I'll tell you, mate. At thirteen I was working the jump-up—stealing parcels off of lorries while drivers had their tea. You never knew what you'd get—a box of toothbrushes, cans of salmon. I once had all the spare parts for a hundred sewing machines. I wasn't hungry—I didn't steal for that. My old man did the best he could for us on whatever he made. But right up to the time when I left home I used to think the rent-collector was one of the family. My mother used to pawn the old man's good suit regular as clockwork every Monday morning. As I say, I was never hungry. But you need a little more than three square meals a day and thieving seemed the only way I could get it. There was a lot in our neighbourhood thought the same. I'll give you a for-instance—how long did you go to school?"

Duncan swallowed the whisky-soda slowly, remembering a succession of ultimatums. ". . . . I must therefore ask you to remove your grandson without further delay . . ." ". . . I regret infinitely that Ritchie must be withdrawn from the school at the end of this current term." RITCHIE ABSCONDED AGAIN STOP POLICE INFORMED STOP PLEASE CABLE INSTRUCTIONS

Bar the last tolerable years in Switzerland, it was a history of loneliness and indiscipline.

"I started at five and finished at twenty," he said. "And

what they did to me shouldn't have been done to a dog. What's that got to do with it?"

Chalice's fist thudded on the table. "Plenty, mate! I'm trying to tell you why I don't turn it up. One of the reason's that I didn't *have* fifteen years schooling. Do you realize I never read a book through till I went inside. I used to think Mozart was a footballer. I had to keep my mouth shut sooner than let people see how stupid I was. I'm still stupid but with a hundred thousand quid people won't mind that. A hundred thousand quid, Ritchie. I'll buy one of them estates over in Ireland and live like a gentleman. I'll read—I might even write the story of my life." He looked challengingly at the Canadian.

"Why not?" Duncan said quietly. It was the thief's green pasture beyond the hill—the prize that once attained would be replaced by another still more illusory. "I wish you luck," he added. "Personally I've kicked the habit. You couldn't tempt me with the keys of the Bank of England."

Chalice worried a piece of loose skin near a nail. "That sounds a funny thing for someone on the run to say."

"Funny" was the wrong adjective. It was completely illogical and yet every word of the statement was true.

"Maybe it does. I just happen to mean what I said. I may be in way over my head but I'm still incorruptible, Harry."

Chalice's face wore an expression of puzzled respect. "You mean all that chat you used to use inside was straight-up— about finding a job, saving your money and moving on? You didn't even know where you were going to move on *to*!"

Duncan thought about it then nodded. "I still don't know, Harry. The only thing I can count on is my fingers. That doesn't necessarily mean that I'm going to hold still while people try to ram my nose into the ground, try to cut me off in my prime. It may seem illogical to you but that's the way it is."

Chalice moved his head in the same grave way as though a major decision had just been taken.

"It's your life, mate. But if you want me to help you, I've got to know something besides two geezers tried to run you down."

Duncan took a deep breath. Whether or not Chalice helped, whatever was said in this room would be held in confidence. His narrative was bald and unemotional.

Chalice listened with his head sunk between his hands. His eyes never left the Canadian's face. Duncan finished wryly.

"I've been handled like a baby, Harry. This girl made a complete sucker out of me. This I don't like. Whatever happens I can't just let it go."

Chalice waited till the next record dropped on the turntable. "I'll tell, Ritchie, I've heard some crap in my time. This beats the lot. I mean, I get these mugs in here trying to put up a piece of business. They tell you what they're supposed to have heard—what they're supposed to have seen. Nine times out of ten it's all bollix. But I've never heard anything stretched this far."

Duncan put his empty glass down very carefully. "Just one thing before you go any farther. I don't like being called a liar."

"Why don't you belt-up?" said Chalice, tapping his forehead. "I'm not talking about you—it's the others. There's something dead-dodgy about this story. Look—all right, this geezer Morgan nicks the film with the bird. Next thing you know he's in the river and she's hearing voices while somebody has a go at you. What you're asking me to believe is that all this is over what's printed on this film. You're saying that it's worth stealing in the first place. It might be—who knows. Maybe Morgan knew where he could take a thing like that. But once you get a coffin in the act, you've got to give me a better reason than a lousy bit of film."

Duncan was overcome by a feeling of intense loneliness. "Can you think of one, Harry? It just might be coincidence that the girl cracked up. Maybe Morgan *did* slip. But when those guys drove that car up on the sidewalk they weren't kidding."

Chalice thumbed out his butt in the ashtray. "Have it your own way, Ritchie. Who *are* these mugs?"

Duncan seized on the word. "Mugs! That's exactly what

you'd call them if you saw them on the street. Only they don't act like mugs, Harry. They're in a racket you probably never even heard of. Industrial spying. The stakes can be so big that they make your bank raids look pitiful. These guys don't have police records, the cops don't know they exist. They don't need to fix things—they just stage them."

Chalice shuttled the idea through his mind. The result seemed to make him dubious.

"What do you mean, 'big stakes'? What do they stand to get out of it?"

Duncan pushed the melted ice round in his glass. He looked up.

"I don't know much about it. But my guess is there could be enough in one take as you need to retire with."

Chalice buttoned his collar and hitched his sweater. "If it's as easy as that, what are we waiting for?"

"It isn't," said Duncan. "You've got to be sure of your market. And your market's got to be sure of you. If we knew where to take that film, I've got a hunch neither of us would see the light of day again."

Chalice knocked rapidly on wood. "Ok—which do you want, help or an opinion, Ritchie?"

"I want both," Duncan said with emphasis. "But I'll settle for either."

Chalice walked as far as the bar, turned and leaned his back against it.

"I'll tell you, Ritchie—if I was in your place I'd be on the first plane out. It wouldn't matter to me *where* it was going. You know why—because you've just convinced me these geezers mean business. Funny to me because I know you won't go. What are you trying to prove?"

Duncan asked himself the same question. How to explain the feeling of anger and frustration—the sense of having been cheated.

"Do you remember what we used to talk about inside, Harry? Why society made laws! You could never understand that laws were for the protection of the minority as well as the majority. If someone breaks in here and steals that record-player or your booze you have the right to call the cops. It doesn't matter that you're a thief yourself or that you wouldn't call them anyway—you have the right. What right have *I* got at this moment? Who's going to listen to me? That's what's getting me, Harry. Society can't have it both ways. I don't care where this girl is, I'm going to get hold of her and she's going to tell me the truth. Why she landed me in all this."

Chalice pursed his lips and blew. The sound was expressive of his thought.

"That'll get you fat, mate! What do you do next—write to the newspapers about it?"

Duncan leant forward. "I don't know that either, Harry. But don't worry about it. I shouldn't have come here in the first place asking for that sort of help. Thanks for the cash and keep whatever I've said under your hat."

Chalice moved swiftly grabbing Duncan by the shoulders and forcing him back in his seat. His face was outraged.

"Where do you think you're going? Look, mate, I'll tell you a little story. A story about someone me and Eddie knows. He's a straight fellow who never had a lot of money —nothing but this florist shop—but he's stood bail for me twice and never asked a penny for it. He got stock about a month ago and borrowed a grand from one of these loan companies. He couldn't pay the money back on time and they wanted to take his business away from him. That's when he told us what had happened, not before. Me and Eddie opened up this office one night, blew the peter and burnt every promissory note and bit of paper in the place. He's still got his shop. All right—he was a mug to borrow money like that but a pal's a pal—whatever he does, Ritchie. What you want me to do?"

It was a while before Duncan trusted himself to answer. "I've got to get to this girl. I'll need transport—I don't know what else till I work out some sort of plan."

Chalice refilled their glasses. His eyes had taken on the narrowed brilliance of a hunter's after game.

"Industrial spying ain't exactly culture but perhaps I'll

still be able to learn something." He started a toneless whistle that had no relation to the tune on the record-player.

Duncan smiled. Chalice had a reputation for carefully-planned strategy.

"I won't forget it, Harry. I might even send you a postcard from Central America."

Chalice grinned. "I don't know what an honest man's going to find round those parts—a medal, maybe. I was only kidding about taking you on the firm, anyway. I can't see you with one of Kathy's stockings over your bonce, swinging a pickaxe handle. Ok. We'll get your gear from the hotel tonight. You can move into my place. We'll send Kathy on a little holiday. First thing tomorrow, we'll get this film back. I want Eddie in on this, Ritchie. Stand on me, he's dead reliable."

The scotch and the other's enthusiasm fired Duncan's resolve.

"Whatever you say," he agreed.

Chalice picked up the bar phone and dialled. "Crying? That's right, still at the club. I don't care who's on telly—get your arse out of bed and over here." He hung up and shook himself like a retriever leaving water. "Inspector Lockhart, he says." He came back to the table. They touched glasses without embarrassment.

Linda Swann

IT was still night-time. This much she knew. Apart from that, she felt as if she had been in the room talking to the two doctors for years. She was comfortable, sitting in a tipped-back chair, watching the smooth cream paint flow over the ceiling and walls. The angles of the desk on the other side of the room were sharp and at the same time distant. The scratch of Doctor Mahler's pen on paper sounded to her like the noise of a bow drawn lightly across violin strings. She was aware, with the back of her head, of the nurse standing behind her—an enormous moth with folded wings.

She opened her handbag in obedience to the soft persuasive voice. She emptied the contents into her lap and explained the purpose of each item. The key—that was for the street door where she lived. They knew about lipstick and eye-liner. There was some money, the wallet with her Faraday pass, insurance cards and Hugh's picture. And the bottle. Her hand started to shake.

Doctor Mahler spoke with intimate understanding. "Don't be frightened, Linda—just put the bottle back in your bag. It's empty. You don't *need* pills to make you sleep—you never did. Who prescribed them for you in the first place?"

She concentrated on the red-bordered label. The name was boldly printed. SOMNADOR. Doctor Mahler turned his desk light out. She drew her knees together, wishing that she could see his face more clearly. It was him she wanted to look at not Frew.

"I don't remember," she whispered.

Doctor Mahler's voice came from the shadows. "It doesn't matter, Linda. You were unhappy—you remember that, don't you? And you went to Doctor Frew. *Why* were you unhappy?"

She looked towards the light. The great hooded bird hopped onto its perch, clinging with ugly curved talons. Its yellow eyes bored into hers, reading her thoughts. Then the bird's head became Frew's. She was restless and hostile. She wanted to punish the bird for knowing everything.

"He locked me up in a room," she said, still whispering. "He's evil."

She started to struggle up from her chair. She was immediately smothered by the warm scented weight of the nurse. Strong hands pushed her down again.

Doctor Mahler spoke reassuringly. "She'll be all right, nurse. Linda, listen to me. Doctor Frew brought you here in his car. It was night-time when you came. What was the first thing you thought of?"

She probed her memory because it was important to him. "I wondered where I was going. I knew that I was being taken somewhere and I felt desperately sorry for myself. Then I came in here and saw you. Everything changed then."

"How did it change?"

A car passed on the street, its headlights sweeping the ceiling. She frowned, momentarily irritated by his lack of understanding.

"You were kind and handsome. Not like him."

The nurse moved, her shadow fluttering on the wall. "Him?" the quiet voice persisted. "Do you mean Doctor Frew?"

She nodded. "He looked like the devil." The bird's head dissolved, its form and colour becoming a twisted stick that jumped as if alive, mocking her.

Doctor Mahler came into the light—a middle-aged man wearing dinner-jacket and cummerbund, cigarette-ash had dropped on his shirt-front. He rubbed the corner of an eye. She had a quick feeling of guilt. He was tired and she was responsible. He came near her chair and put his hand on her shoulder.

"You were crying just a little while ago, Linda. What was it that was making you so unhappy?"

She brushed the falling hair from in front of her face and told him.

"My thoughts come too fast. I can't keep up with them."

She heard Frew's chair rasp across the floor, the rustle of papers. She shut her eyes. The next time she opened them, he was standing where Mahler had been. He put a pencil and pad in her lap.

"Write something, Linda—your name."

She hung her head obstinately. "You *know* I can't. My hands are too heavy."

A clock ticked through the silence. Frew returned to his seat. The expanse of paper across her knees was vast and forbidding. She was grateful that Mahler helped her.

"Draw something, Linda," he encouraged. "You liked drawing when you were little, didn't you?"

She smiled for him and picked up the pencil. She drew a circle and stared down at it, smiling secretly.

"That's time. I'm running round in it like a needle in a gramophone record." She added two loops, one each side of the circle. "And those are my hands. But they unbalance me—can you see that?"

Frew's voice seemed to sound in an echo-chamber. "How about Hugh, Linda. Do you still love him or do you hate him now? He stole something that belonged to you, didn't he?"

Part of her mind rebelled violently against the suggestion. They didn't know it but for Hugh she could still be cunning and convincing.

"That wasn't Hugh at all. He didn't even know. It was the other man—the Canadian."

Frew's voice persisted. "He didn't even know what?"

"Things," she said after a while. "Just things."

"But there isn't a Canadian, not really, is there?" Frew asked insinuatingly. Hugh and the Canadian are the same man, really, aren't they, Linda? That's what you told me yesterday, remember? You said that he stole something belonging to you and then you came to see me. He found out where you were and told me to put drugs in your food. That's really why you hate him, isn't it?"

She felt like a small animal at bay with the great bird hunting her.

"No!" she cried in a loud voice. "It's not true. I don't hate anyone except myself and you."

The nurse drifted behind her. Linda reached up, imprisoning the woman's wrists. The nurse bent down, making soothing noises.

"Take him away," whispered Linda. "He's hurting me."

The lines round Mahler's mouth and eyes distressed her. She felt that she was letting him down and wanted to be alone with him to explain. Her fear of Frew was now secondary to her anxiety for Mahler's approval.

"What are you thinking about now—this very minute?" he asked softly.

She burst into an involuntary fit of weeping, revolted by the idea of making him share her anguish. She blotted her tears with her handkerchief and tried desperately for self-possession.

"You two," she said simply. "This room—what you think of me. I believe that my spirit will soon be free and my body won't matter. I'll have done exactly what you think is impossible. I'll *be* shapes and colours—*be* the way things feel."

She took the glass Frew gave her and drank, emotionally drained and exhausted. Nothing mattered. All she had to do was concentrate until the weight of the chains dropped. Not until then would she really be part of the stars and the sky. She was dimly aware of the two men talking—of the nurse wrapping her in blankets. She stretched out on the couch and after a while slept.

She woke with a strong impression of being watched. She struggled up in the narrow bed, clutching the neck of the flannel night-gown. Day had been breaking when she had come to this place. She remembered the drive from London through a countryside still in the November dawn. She looked round the room. There was a plain deal table with drawers by the side of her bed, a chair. A plastic screen in the corner half-concealed a lavatory and shower. She saw nothing in the room that belonged to her. The candy-striped tunic lying on the chair was new. On top of it were bra, pants and a pair of nylons. Heel-less slippers were pushed under the chair.

She swung her feet from the bed to the ground. The floor was covered with sisal matting reaching from one distempered wall to the other. She put her hand against a duct above her head. A current of warm air blew against it. The inside of the door was lined with a sheet of painted metal. There was no handle. The window was set abnormally high —on a level with the top of her head. It was impossible to see out. She dragged a chair over and stood on it. The panes of glass were a quarter-inch thick. The top of the window lowered outwards but only for a few inches. Iron stays prevented further movement. Beyond the damp grass and flower-beds outside was a high wall topped with spikes. The trees and the garden had the moist peaceful look of early morning. Sparrows squabbled over crumbs underneath the neighbouring window. She jumped down, staring about her in sudden panic. Then she ran to the door and started pounding on it with her fists. Somebody along the passage took up the banging. A woman shrieked—another broke into a high, keening wail.

Linda's fists beat frantically. She was conscious of her own voice screaming, louder than anyone else's. She stopped suddenly and leant her forehead against the steel-lined door. She must find something she could use to smash the window with. She pulled the drawer from the table, climbed back on the chair and started hammering on the pane with the corner of the drawer. The glass sang under the blows but nevertheless held.

All at once the door was thrown open. A nurse in grey uniform came in. She shot the spring lock so that the door could not slam and imprison her on the wrong side. She had a firm voice that was not unkindly. She spoke as though she had said the same thing many many times before.

"Get down from the window, dear. You'll catch your death of cold running about with no clothes on."

Linda jumped down, shrinking against the wall. The nurse paid no attention to her but fussed with the bed, straightening the sheets and blankets. She patted the pillow encouragingly.

"Come along, dear. Do as you're told. We certainly don't want to make things difficult for other people, do we?"

Linda shook her head. She must be calm and act sensibly. Above all no hysterics.

"I'd like to see the doctor immediately, nurse, please. Will you tell him that I *must* see him—now."

The nurse threw back the bedclothes. "Of course I will, dear. But it's early—not even seven o'clock. Get back into bed and we'll see about some breakfast for you."

Linda lay down, compressing herself into as little space

106

as possible. She stared up into a pale patient face that would be proof against all fantasy. The nurse was in her forties with muscular arms and legs.

"Please listen to me," Linda said quickly. "Just tell me what this place is—I've *got* to know where they brought me—don't you see that?"

The nurse settled the pillow more comfortably under Linda's head.

"There's haddock for breakfast. Which do you want to drink—tea, coffee or milk?"

She lifted herself on an elbow. "It's a prison, isn't it?" she challenged. "But I haven't *done* anything, nurse!"

The woman's face wore a shocked expression. "A prison! What a dreadful thing to say, Linda. People love you—they want to see you get well. Suppose they heard you say a thing like that—imagine how unhappy it would make them feel."

Linda ran her tongue over dry lips. An unpleasant taste lingered in her mouth. She remembered her arrival dimly. The doctors, huddled together on the lighted steps, talking. Doctor Mahler's face—the one she had thought was her friend. The memory was vague as if it had all happened very long ago. She began to feel desperate but exposed the flaw in the woman's argument without raising her voice.

"But I *am* well, nurse. There's been a mistake. That's why I must see the doctor immediately and explain everything. It's all very simple really. I just have to explain."

The nurse touched Linda's cheek with a warm hand smelling of soap.

"I know, dear. But first you have to rest. I promise you'll see doctor later." She rummaged in her apron pocket and found a thermometer. She flicked down the mercury, smiling confidentially.

Linda's lips closed on the slender glass tube. The crack in the door revealed a stretch of white-painted passage, a red fire-extinguisher hanging on a hook. The nurse plumped down on the bed. By tilting her head, Linda was able to read the pad on the nurse's knee.

BRIERLEY MENTAL NURSING HOME

ROOM	NAME OF PATIENT	AGE	REMARKS
4	SWANN, LINDA	28	No barbiturates

The nurse took the thermometer reading. "There," she said brightly. "You couldn't be healthier. Now we're going to rest until breakfast and then have a nice hot shower."

Linda closed her eyes obediently. For the time being she must do everything that they said—play the part they expected of her. When the doctor came he would find her perfectly calm and relaxed. He'd know immediately that a mistake had been made. Instinct told her that she mustn't say anything about Frew until she was out of this place. Just that she'd been unhappy and upset and that now she was over it. Of *course*, they'd understand. After all, she was only there for observation in any case. All they had to do was listen to her—look at her—to realize the truth.

She sat up with a profound sense of shock, remembering Hugh and the film. Where could she go—who could she turn to—who would believe her? She heard her own voice as it had been in Doctor Mahler's consulting room— positive and. preposterous. She recalled the circle she had drawn and ridiculously called "time". These were the thoughts of an unbalanced person. *Her* thoughts—and people would know it.

She carried her knuckles to her mouth, her face crumpling. She flung herself down again and covered her head with the pillow. She lay in this position for what seemed like a long time. Without tears, numbed and defenceless.

She heard a door open somewhere along the passage—a trolley bumping against the wall. She sat up, combing her hair as best she could with her fingers and composing herself. She would be like a prisoner preparing his escape, a model of good behaviour. Later on they'd let her into the garden—she'd find a way out and run. She didn't know where but she'd run. She was smiling as the door opened.

A negress with thick spectacles wheeled in a food trolley. The same nurse lifted a tray onto Linda's lap.

"There. Now eat up like a good girl then make yourself pretty for the doctor," she said good-naturedly.

Coffee was served in a carton. Plates, knife and fork were fashioned out of some grey plastic material. The food was plain but appetising. Linda undid her paper napkin.

"How am I supposed to make myself presentable. There isn't even a mirror."

"Nonsense," the nurse said briskly. She rattled the shower-curtain along the rail. A stainless steel plate with brightly polished surface was let into the wall. A selection of brushes, soap and tooth-paste were in a niche below. "You don't look, do you," she chided. She took a cardboard-box from the tray and put it on the table. "Here's something to pass the time away with." She spread a rubber mat across the bottom of the shower and tested the hot water. Her back was turned to the bed.

Linda looked at the orderly, trying to establish communication. The negress's eyes rolled behind her spectacles. She wheeled the trolley hurriedly outside. Once alone, Linda showered and dressed herself in the striped tunic. She stood in front of the mirror trying to see herself as a stranger would. Head held high, her pale lips parted, a confident expression in her eyes. She dragged her hair back from her forehead. It was no good. She was a bad actress. Her face showed the very emotions they would expect to find—guilt and fear. She undid the cardboard box that the nurse had left. The jigsaw puzzle was of odd design. The coloured label offered four different solutions—each had several common factors. A man, a woman, a wooden house burning among the trees, a lake and a road leading away from the scene. The first picture portrayed the man and woman carrying buckets of water in the direction of the flames. In the second, both were on the road and hurrying away from the house. The third showed the man walking towards the lake, leaving the woman by the blazing building. The last reversed these positions. Some of the pieces were two-sided so that they might be used in alternative fashion.

She flung the puzzle down angrily. She had no intention of meeting that sort of nonsense halfway. She started pacing the floor from door to window and back, stopping now and then to put her ear against the door and listen. When she heard footsteps in the corridor she ran to her chair and sat down primly with legs crossed, waiting for the door to be undone. The nurse came in first, closing the shower-curtains, shaking her head at the water-splashed matting.

"Say good morning to the doctor, Linda," she said mechanically, folded her hands on her stomach and smiled.

Linda stood on legs that wavered as much as her voice. "Good morning, doctor."

He was a head shorter than the nurse with neat white hair and a chicken-neck. His small mouth was pursed importantly. He wore a white linen coat over dark trousers and trotted rather than walked. He took her wrist, feeling her pulse but she knew he was looking at the faint webbing of scars. Stiff grey eyebrows formed a frieze over eyes that were never still.

"I see that you're bored with the puzzle. I'm not surprised. Idiotic things. How did you sleep?"

His manner gave her confidence. "I've got to talk to you in private, doctor. Immediately. It can't wait."

He dropped her hand and nodded. "I don't think I've seen this patient's admittal papers, have I, sister?"

The nurse glanced at him significantly. "No, doctor. Nurse Trelawney was on duty when she arrived. She left word that Doctor Evans wanted to speak to you about the case."

The doctor dredged an old-fashioned watch from an inside pocket, with a length of gold chain.

"Yes, I understand." He smiled at Linda, showing teeth stained with tobacco. "You wanted to talk to me—what about?"

She looked at the small mouth framing its wet smile and felt lost. In spite of it, she kept a firm hold on herself.

"It's very simply really, doctor. I understand that I'm being kept here for mental observation. Is that correct?"

The doctor's brown eyes were guarded. "You're here for treatment," he corrected.

"Do you mind telling me on what authority?" She asked steadily.

He teetered on the balls of his feet, his face grown red and testy. He looked as though he had been asked the same question too many times and was tired of it.

"On the recommendation of two medical practitioners, Miss Swann. One who certainly had previous acquaintance with you—the other who had special experience in the diagnosis of mental disorder. And if you're prepared to act like the sensible young lady I'm sure you really are, we'll have you out of here in double-quick time."

Her control snapped under the finality in his voice. She dodged past the nurse's restraining arm.

"You're a liar! There *is* no doctor who knows me! It's a plot and unless you listen to me you'll be part of it! Do you understand that—part of a plot to keep me here illegally!"

The doctor skipped backwards, putting the nurse between Linda and himself. He spoke over his shoulder as he left the room.

"I'll see her later, sister." His footsteps tapped away along the passage.

The nurse's bosom swelled. "You ought to be thoroughly ashamed of yourself," she said censoriously.

Linda was still shaking. "You get this into your head, you horrible old hag—I'm *not* insane and I'm *not* here legally. I'm going to see that you get into trouble with the rest of them. Now I demand paper and a pen and some envelopes. I want to write some letters."

The nurse took a deep breath. Her pale face had flushed. She seemed on the verge of saying something but left the room, slamming the door violently. She was back within minutes, throwing writing materials on the bed contemptuously. She handed a printed card to Linda, her voice tart.

"Read that before you start writing your letters."

She went out again. The card was explicit.

BRIERLEY MENTAL NURSING HOME

Rules for the guidance of patients' correspondence
(Extracts from Mental Health Act, 1959)

36 (1) Any postal packet addressed to a patient detained in a hospital under this Part of this Act may be withheld from the patient if, in the opinion of the responsible medical officer, the receipt of the packet would be calculated to interfere with the treatment of the patient or to cause him unnecessary distress: and any packet so withheld shall, if the name and address of the sender are sufficiently identified therein, be returned to him by post.

(2) Subject to the provisions of this section, any postal packet addressed by a patient so detained and delivered by him for dispatch may be withheld from the Post Office—

(a) if the addressee has given notice in writing to the managers of the hospital or to the responsible medical officer requesting that communications addressed to him by the patient should be withheld; or

(b) if it appears to that officer that the packet would be unreasonably offensive to the addressed, or is defamatory of other persons (other than persons on the staff of the hospital) or would be likely to prejudice the interests of the patient. Provided that this subsection does not apply to any postal packet addressed as follows, that is to say—

(1) to the Minister;

(2) to any Member of the Commons House of Parliament;

(3) to the Master or Deputy-Master or any other officer of the Court of Protection;

(4) to the managers of the hospital;

(5) to any other authority or person having power to discharge the patient under this Part of this Act;

(6) at any time when the patient is entitled to make application to a Mental Health Review Tribunal, to that tribunal, and regulations made by the Minister may except from this subsection, subject to such conditions or limitations (if any) as may be prescribed by the regulations, postal packets addressed to such other classes of persons as may be so prescribed.

She put the card down, her mind fogged. "Unreasonably offensive." ". . . the interests of the patient . . ." "Conditions, limitations, (if any)." The words made no sense. She wrote three letters and sealed the envelopes. Lunch came later, well-cooked steak, stringbeans and fried potatoes, a sweet and a glass of fruit juice. The nurse took the letters, her face stony with disapproval. Lunch over, Linda drank her juice and lay down, staring at the ceiling. As the shapes in the room began to distort, she started giggling. The ceiling became remote. She drifted, still laughing but with a feeling of intense and utter release.

Ritchie Duncan

CRYING Eddie was lying on his back, glumly considering the elegance of his handmade shoes. He wore charcoal-grey trousers and a dark wool shirt. A rolled-up suede jacket supported his head. A couple of tufts of shortish blond hair gave him the look of a lynx disturbed in its lair. He switched his stare from Chalice to Duncan and then back again.

"We're going in *where*?" he demanded.

"A mental nursing-home," Duncan repeated. "An asylum if you prefer it."

113

Way below the penthouse windows, the lamps of the Outer Circle followed the perimeter of Regent's Park. The long room they were sitting in was red carpeted. White-painted shelves against the end walls were stacked with an indiscriminate array of books. *The Encyclopaedia Britannica, Simenon, Pond's Book of Etiquette, Law for the Layman, Ruff's Guide to the Turf* and a complete set of *Chandler*, bound in hand-tooled leather. The chairs and sofa were covered with a checked material. A large grey parrot perched on a stand by the window, its leg fastened by a chain. Chalice handed the bird a nut that it cracked with its powerful bill. It turned a cautious eye on Chalice and asked the question in a disturbingly natural voice.

"Guilty or not guilty, mate?"

Crying Eddie sat up, hugging his knees. "That bloody bird's beginning to give me the creeps. One of these days I'm going to wring its neck. Did you hear what the man just said, Harry. An asylum."

Chalice scratched the parrot's poll. "That's right. What's the matter, don't you like the idea?"

Eddie rocked to and fro. "I think it's great. I'm clapping myself stupid."

There was an ice-bucket on the floor, filled with cola bottles. Chalice selected one and tossed it at Crying Eddie.

"Why don't you belt up! You're making us nervous. Get drunk and relax. OK. Ritchie, show us where this gaff is."

Duncan leant over the large-scale ordnance map. He traced the way into Ascot with a forefinger. Brierley Mental Nursing Home was shown in a wood near the race-track.

"The road finishes at the asylum—do you see that? There's no other way to get near the place except through the trees."

Chalice scowled. "Exactly the set-up that I don't like. I've had trouble every time I've been lumbered with one of these dead-ends. Some bastard comes up and parks in front of you or behind and you can't get out. That reminds me—what are we going to use to get down there?"

Duncan looked up. "Not a hired car, that's for sure. They

114

want to see an operator's licence—they remember your face."

Chalice discarded the suggestion. "I know that, mate. We'll take the Jag. If there's any dodgy business later, Crying can pick up a car in Ascot."

Crying Eddie offered the room a tortured grin. " 'Crying can pick up a car,' " he mimicked. "The Master-mind at work again. You ought to be on television."

Chalice ignored him. "This Brierley Nursing Home looks a fair size, Ritchie—all them grounds and things. How do we find where this bird is—knock on the door and ask?"

Duncan folded the map and put it back in the bookcase. He turned round slowly.

"There's no 'we' about it, Harry. All you do is take me there. I do the rest."

Chalice's expression was dubious. "What happens if you get close enough to see her but you can't talk—what do you do, wave?"

Duncan's face hardened. "I'll bring her out with me."

"What and walk home?" Chalice continued. "You're as nutty as a fruit-cake yourself, Ritchie. What do you think me and Crying's going to be there for—the exercise?"

Crying Eddie rolled over on his side. He affected great interest in the twin walkie-talkie sets on the floor beside him. He fiddled with the controls and spoke stiffly into the air.

"Calling all cars—calling all cars! Four lunatics at large, last seen near Ascot Racecourse. Break out your butterfly nets and close in on them."

The nasal monotone appeared to excite the parrot. It chattered its beak the length of its chain. Chalice walked over and removed the walkie-talkie sets from Crying Eddie's grasp.

"Why don't you bugger off?" he asked sombrely. "Go home to bed and watch Inspector Lockhart. That's more your idea than helping your mates. Go on, get lost. I'd sooner have Kathy on the job. She don't worry."

Crying Eddie gave him the two-finger sign and sank back

on the sofa, shutting his eyes. Chalice draped a cloth over the parrot and walked a few steps, whistling tonelessly. He stopped, smiling as if he had just remembered something long-since forgotten.

"I've got it, Ritchie. You bring the bird here. She can sleep on the sofa unless you've got other ideas for her."

Duncan looked at him steadily. "I've got no other ideas. She can sleep in Kathy's bed—I'll take the sofa and thanks, Harry."

Chalice glanced at his watch. "It's pretty near nine. How long's it going to take us to get down there, Crying?"

Crying Eddie came to life, answering with a professional assessment of time, distance and traffic hazards.

"About forty minutes. Bayswater, Shepherd's Bush, the Uxbridge Road and out through Chiswick. Then straight down the A4. If we're lucky it might be a bit less."

Chalice opened a drawer in an inlaid bureau. He took the small black book to the phone and switched on a goose-necked lamp. He found a number in the book and then dialled.

"Is that Phil Gelb? It's Harryboy, Phil. Look we're going to be on your manor tonight. If the law stops us I'm saying that we're on our way to you. There's three of us—Crying, me and another geezer. You're giving a party for us, Phil. A *party*! I don't know why, that's up to you—you're just *giving* it. There's nothing dodgy about it, no. We're just making a social call." He thudded the heel of his hand against his forehead and bawled at the top of his voice. "A SOCIAL CALL, Phil. So long, mate, and be lucky."

He cradled the receiver and stretched his legs, yawning. "That's Phil Gelb. He used to manage Selby and them good fighters. He's got a pub near Maidenhead. I just wanted to make sure that we've got a reason for being on the manor if we should run into any patrols. Come to think of it, if the cops ever should phone Phil, God help them. He wears one of those hearing-aids. Half the time he doesn't get what you're saying because he says he hears radio programmes." He prodded Crying Eddie with his toe. "Come on, dreamer."

Crying Eddie rose like a good sport cornered. Chalice looked at Duncan's grey flannel suit speculatively.

"You're supposed to know about this lark, Ritchie, but I thought you wore dark clothes, creeping about people's houses. No?"

Crying Eddie shrugged into his suede jacket and smoothed his hair down.

"He means why don't you be like him, Canada. As soon as Harry pulls something over his head he thinks he's invisible."

"Very funny," Chalice said absent-mindedly. "What's the matter, don't you want to . . ."

". . . grow up and have troubles," Crying Eddie finished for him. "No, mate. I've got my share already."

Duncan wriggled his shoulders. "I'd be wearing dark clothes if I had any, Harry. You saw me unpack."

Chalice went through to his bedroom. He came back and dumped an assortment of garments on the sofa.

"Try these. If anyone asks what you're doing tell 'em you're bird watching."

Duncan emptied his pockets, taking nothing with him but a few bills and some change. The dark-blue ski trousers and sweater fitted him comfortably. He laced on black basket-ball boots and straightened up.

"I'm ready whenever you are."

Chalice took one last look round the room, adjusting the cover over the parrot's perch. He nodded at the walkie-talkie sets slung from Eddie's shoulder.

"We've used those a couple of times already. Me and Crying wouldn't be without 'em on business now. Do you know how to work them, Ritchie?"

Duncan took the small set Crying Eddie handed him. It was the size and weight of a small transistor radio.

"Japanese," said Chalice. "They've got a range of half-a-mile and you can't go wrong with them."

He cut the lights in the apartment. They left through the kitchen, reaching the back of the building by the fire-escape.

It was almost ten as they drove into Ascot. They cruised

about the town till Chalice found the beam-and-plaster inn he was looking for. He touched Crying Eddie's arm, signalling towards the car-park.

"Drive in there, mate, and get as close to the windows as you can."

The Jaguar rustled over the gravelled approach and on to the concrete lot. Crying Eddie cut the motor, leaning forward and peering up through the windows. The bar inside was softly lighted with well-polished woodwork and the glint of silver. A redheaded girl with bare shoulders was playing Shearing type piano.

Crying Eddie rubbed his palms together briskly. "That'll do me—standing in front of the fire chatting up that bird."

Chalice looked at him scornfully. "With a lemonade in your fork? Birds like that prefer the older type of man. Besides that you'd be out of place. This is where country gentlemen go—stockbrokers and people. You'd be talking out the side of your mouth and frightening them. Anyway, you got work to do." He unfastened the dash-compartment and pulled out a canvas roll. He handed it to Duncan together with one of the walkie-talkie sets. "I'll be in the pub if you want me. All you got to do is call in every quarter-of-an-hour. If you skip one period, that's OK. Skip two and me and Eddie'll bring the car down to the bottom of that road."

Duncan slung the set from his shoulder. "What happens if I skip three of them?"

Chalice's badger-head nodded assurance. "We'll be wherever you are, mate, whacking about. Look after yourself and don't take no stupid chances."

Duncan pushed the canvas roll down inside his trousers. "This place shuts around eleven. I may be longer."

"We'll still be here," Chalice answered. "We'll change a wheel or something. You came here with us and you'll go back with us."

He swivelled the driving-mirror round, trying out a couple of slow smiles, eyes hooded. The next they saw of him was through the window, carrying a drink across to the girl at the piano. She looked up at him, smiling welcome.

Crying Eddie grunted. "I'd give a fifty to see Kathy walk in on him now. Ah, well—we'd better get going. What time have you got?"

They synchronized watches. The other cars in the parking-lot were empty. Duncan opened his door, aware of what was behind the other man's brief handshake. This was the hard core of comradeship—critical yet loyal to a degree unimaginable to those beyond its closed circle. He walked across the dark expanse of tarmac and turned left up the unlighted road. It ran between hedged fields with here and there a house set well back, remote from the highway. After a while, he broke into a trot, his rubber-shod feet soundless on the hardtop surface. The night was starless and sharp with the promise of more ground-frost. A hint of burning leaves hung in the air. He ran with eyes and ears alert for the first sign of danger. Strangers would be suspect in a locality like this. A chance pair of lovers, a man walking his dog, might mean a telephone call to the police. The equipment he was carrying would be enough for even a country cop to hold him.

A quarter-mile away, a sign-post glimmered at the junction. He shone his pencil flash on it. PRIVATE ROAD BRIERLEY MENTAL NURSING HOME ONLY. He forced his way through the hawthorn hedge and broke for the shelter of the trees ahead, stumbling over the hardening furrows. He stopped at the edge of the wood, looking right towards the gates of the asylum. They were tall and set in a high brick wall. Ten acres had been gouged out of the middle of the beech wood and enclosed by the wall. A deep hush lay over everything. Once into the trees, it was even stiller—darker. He had the feeling of being shadowed by unseen animals. Once a bird blundered out of the branches, raucous with fright. A smell of rotting wood rose underfoot, the astringency of crushed ivy. Suddenly he walked into wire. His trousers tore in the first frantic struggle to free himself. He felt his way along the strands of barbed wire to their anchorage in the nearest tree. He went back in the opposite direction. The entire wood was ringed with loops and spans of snagged rusty wire, impossible to jump or crawl under. He squatted down and unzipped the suede case. He watched the second-hand on his watch. As it hit the quarter-hour, he snapped down the button. He spoke quietly and distinctly.

"I'm in the woods about a hundred yards from the front gates. The whole place looks dead to me and as far as I can see there's no back way in. I'll have to go over the wall. There's wire everywhere. I'm cutting it. Over."

He fumbled hurriedly with the volume control as Crying Eddie's voice crackled in the trees.

"All right, mate. Keep moving. Everything's in order this end. He's still in there larking about with that bird. If he closes his eyes any more he won't be able to see. Over and out."

Duncan switched off and pulled out the canvas roll. He used the strong pliers on the wire and dragged the loose strands to one side. The brick wall was twenty yards ahead through the trees. He ran to it and marked a spot in direct line with the gap he had cut in the wire. If he had to leave in a hurry, he wanted to be able to stay on his feet. There was a clearing between the wood and the wall—a few feet overgrown with moss and weeds. He took the narrow avenue as far as the front gates. A wicket was set in the left-hand panel —a couple of bells in the gate post. One was labelled VISITORS, the other EMERGENCY. He trotted back to the place he'd marked and undid the canvas roll again. The equipment was Chalice's contribution—ordered by phone with the nonchalant certainty of a Bond Street shopper, fetched and paid for by Crying Eddie. Duncan's impression had been that an order for a hundredweight of gelignite would have been filled with as much ease and as little comment. The aluminium rod was telescopic, extending twenty times its own length. A catch on its end fitted into a ring attached to a slender nylon rope. The rope was knotted every couple of feet to give purchase. He fastened the rope to the rod, reached up and hooked the line over the top of the wall. He freed the rod and retracted its length to a barrel no more than a foot long. The rope supported his weight without stretching. He went up, climbing hand over hand. He straddled the wall at the top and surveyed the scene on the other side.

The two-storey structure was smaller than he had expected and built in the shape of a fat T. The lateral bar faced the massive gates. Lights shone from various windows in a haphazard way, establishing no definite pattern. The front of the building had a covered balcony, draped with creeper. A few beeches that had been spared spread bare branches over the tattered lawns. He lowered himself to the ground, unhooked the rope and stowed everything back in the canvas roll. He circled the chrysanthemum beds and made for the rear of the building. The unmistakable odour of institutional cooking led him to the kitchen. He crept close to the window. The cement floor inside was wet as though it had recently been hosed. Metal sinks and food-trolleys reflected the cold strip-lighting in the ceiling. There was a coffee-pot percolating on one of the stoves but nobody was in the kitchen. He ducked under the sill and moved as far as the door. It opposed the pressure of his shoulder. He tried top and bottom with a gloved hand. Resistance was strong at both levels. Experience told him that the door was bolted as well as locked. He went on round the corner, past galvanized swill-tubs to a large garage. He shone his flash through the dusty panes. The small circle of light picked out the lines of a white-painted ambulance. He had described a wide arc, passing from one side of the building to the other.

The darkness here was intensified by the blaze from the front of the building. As soon as his eyes focused, he made out ten first-floor windows, each placed unnaturally high in the wall. Like the window in a prison-cell. He saw the ventilation flaps that lowered on iron brackets. A feeling of claustrophobia punched itself into his consciousness. He was suddenly very aware of the tall closed gates and silent encircling wood.

He hurtled sideways as someone within the building burst out laughing. It was a strange sound, without mirth and utterly unnerving. He swallowed hard, looking across at the wall. It wasn't too late to call it a day and pull out. Harry and Crying Eddie would be waiting for him back in town. If he went now, they could have a drink together in the pub —another hour and they'd be in London. After a while, the whole episode would begin to seem unreal—a tale of near-disaster told a little smugly among good friends. And yet so much would be missing from the tale. How tell of a rejection that spread like a virus through three generations of a family, crystallizing in the attitude of the society they all professed to believe in. Even the slogan of their kind destroyed you before you started—*the leopard never changes its spots*. Surely he had the right, just once, to force them all out into the open. To say to them in effect that this time the rules were theirs and he'd played them.

The canvas roll had slipped a little. He tightened his belt and walked determinedly to the front of the building. A square of macadam extended from the entrance gates to a flight of stone steps up to the balcony. He padded across and ran the length of the façade preceded by his shadow. The last window was open at the top. He stood against the wall, peering through the curtain of creeper that surrounded the frame. A newspaper rustled inside. He heard the sound of a man clearing his throat noisily. He came a little nearer. The office was divided by a broad counter with a bench on one side. On the other was a desk, telephone switchboard and an elderly man sitting in a cane chair. He was reading a newspaper and warming his feet. Through the open door on the visitors' side was a glimpse of highly-polished floor and aseptic walls with fire-extinguishers hanging on them. A loud clock ticked over the switchboard.

Duncan moved away, holding his breath. He vaulted the front of the balcony and retreated into the shadows till he was a hundred yards from the nursing-home. His watch showed the quarter-hour coming up in a couple of minutes. He unslung the two-way radio, thumbing the catch up and down impatiently as he tried for a response. He cut into Crying Eddie's answer.

"Listen—I've got to take a chance. Get hold of Harry and tell him to call the nursing-home. He asks for Linda Swann. Say he's a cousin or something with a very important message—he must speak to her. I can see the guy who's operating the switchboard. It's just possible that I can get a lead from what he does. If that doesn't work, I'll have to think again. There are rooms all over the place—she could be in any one of them. Is that clear, Crying? Tell him to phone right away. I'll call you back immediately. Over."

He throttled the volume and held the set to his ear. The metallic whisper was faint.

"I'll get him now. You're sure you know what you're doing?"

He switched off, leaving the question unanswered and strapped the small box round his waist. He had to have his arms and legs free yet dared not dump any of the equipment. He crossed the lawns, certain that he was alone in the gloom of the garden. He climbed back onto the balcony, avoiding the lighted stretch in front of the steps. He crouched by the window, sweating heavily, his ears strained for the sound of the telephone buzzer. It came more quickly than he expected. He inched to the window and parted the creeper.

The old man gathered himself together methodically, removing his spectacles and folding his newspaper. Each movement seemed to take an age. Duncan's mouth worked silently. The old fool was senile. If he didn't answer soon Chalice might well hang up. But the buzzer repeated its summons. The old man settled himself at the switchboard and adjusted the headphones.

"Brierley Mental Nursing Home. This is the night-porter speaking."

The creeper rustled gently as Duncan pushed his head forward. He drew back, convinced that the porter would have heard the slight movement. But the man was conscious of nothing except what was in his headphones. He rotated a board that looked like a display-stand for postcards and ran a thumbnail underneath an entry.

"Miss Swann, sir? I'm very much afraid I can't help you. None of the patients is allowed to take telephone calls, you see. And the night-nurse is having her supper. If the message is important why don't you . . ." He broke off, looking down at the mouthpiece in his hand with an air of bewilderment.

Duncan frowned. Chalice ought to have left some name instead of just hanging up. The porter would think it strange. He lifted his head again. The old man turned away from the switchboard, mumbling to himself. He collected his spectacles and newspaper and settled back in his chair. Duncan retreated to the bushes and unfastened the two-way radio set.

"It just might work, Crying. This is what you do—drive down Hollister till you reach a signpost on your left. It's all clearly marked on the map. Then one of you gets out and walks down to the gates. *Walk*—don't bring the car. You'll see a couple of bells. One's marked EMERGENCY. Ring it and get into the trees right away. Ok? Down Hollister, left at the signpost and ring the bell. If this works I won't call in again for half-an-hour. Over and out."

He rose from his crouch, his hands nervous with zips and straps. Lights had come on to the right in the apartments over the garage. He watched a uniformed nurse appear at the window, her fingers trailing across the forehead. Her voice was clear as she called to someone behind her in the room. Then she drew the curtains. He found himself tiptoeing away, the shirt he was wearing under the sweater cold and damp on his ribs. Why would that woman be bawling about the place with patients sleeping only a few yards away—unless to give him a false sense of security. He imagined the darkened sections of the building peopled with figures—the porter settled back impassively in his chair waiting for the next move. Yet keyed-up nerves had betrayed him before—he mustn't let it happen again.

He ran as far as the front gates and examined the wicket. It was secured by a simple spring lock. He slid the catch back. The small door opened easily. He closed it without sound. He circled the lighted part of the courtyard as far

124

as the end of the balcony. He was getting the hang of things now—a quick grab at the balustrade, a heave and roll took him almost underneath the porter's window. He inched along to his vantage-point. The man was dozing in his chair, his eyes half-closed, his newspaper on the ground beside him.

Duncan picked up the throaty murmur of twin exhausts a quarter-of-a-mile away. His ears followed the course of the Jaguar till it stopped at the T-junction. He started to count the seconds. Whichever of them was going to ring the bell had a hundred and fifty yards to cover. Half-a-minute went by. The sudden sound split the silence—a strident ringing somewhere inside the building. It rang three times in quick succession, echoing through the empty offices. The porter jerked upright and looked about him in bewildered fashion. Then he hurried into the hall. As Duncan heard the doors being opened, he threw up the window and swung his legs over the sill. By the time the porter started across the court-yard, Duncan had lowered the window again and was standing by the switchboard. He turned the revolving stand. The entry he was looking for was halfway down the alphabetical list.

OBSERVATION ROOM 4 SWANN, Linda. (Doctor Wilson.)

He ducked under the counter into the hall, sweating again and drymouthed as he waited there apprehensively. Through the half-open door he could see the porter shuffling towards the wicket-gate. Duncan dropped on all fours, moving backwards to the far side of the hall. His rubbersoled boots left tracks on the polished boards. He wiped these off as he went with his handkerchief. He crawled past a swing door labelled STAFF ONLY. Instinct told him that this was to be avoided. He chose another door on the other side and came to his feet, head swinging like a fighting-bull facing danger. He groped behind his back for the handle and turned it. He stepped into an unlighted office and closed the door again. The window was a pale patch in the darkness. He tiptoed over and looked out. The porter was coming up the steps leading to the balcony, mumbling and muttering. Duncan shifted to the door, putting an ear to the crack, his fingers ready to turn the key on the inside.

Seconds later, a woman's footsteps clattered in the entrance-hall. He heard her strong Northern Irish accent. "What in the name of God was all that about, George? Half-past ten at night, no less, with the difficult ones sleeping!"

The porter's mumble sharpened into complaint. "You *know* what it was—the Emergency bell rung again. I don't get paid to deal with the likes of them hooligans. Didn't they do the same thing only two weeks ago, only then it was past midnight. Doctor Peebles promised he was going to talk to the police about it. And what *did* he do—nothing!"

The nurse's voice soothed him. "He did so, you disbelieving old fellow, you. The sergeant knows who it is—the louts from the building site up on Hollister Road. He'll teach a few of them a sharp lesson, you can be sure of it. Now have you had your coffee yet, George?"

The porter's tone was unsoftened. "No I haven't. One of these nights I'm going to disconnect that bell and we'll see what happens then."

The nurse sounded shocked. "Indeed and you'll do no such thing. Those lads'll not be back again. Just read your newspaper like a good man and I'll fetch your coffee. Isn't it the lucky man you are, waited on hand and foot and me the only one on night-duty."

"Three spoonfuls of sugar," the old man said slyly. "You'd think that Nurse Baxter bought it out of her own pocket, the way she dishes it out. There's one that would have made a good wife. By the way, somebody was on the telephone asking for number 4. A man. He wouldn't leave a message and I didn't catch his name."

The nurse's reply was inaudible. Her feet recrossed the hall, the sound diminishing as she went through the pass-door. He felt his way cautiously across the room, the searcher in an eerie game of hide-and-go-seek. His outstretched hands touched a roll-top desk. He turned his flash on it. There were three envelopes in a tray marked PATIENTS

MAIL, OUTGOING. He picked up the top one. It was addressed to a firm of insurance-brokers in the City, someone had pencilled the digit 4 where the stamp would be stuck. The second bore the name Major Philip Sangster in care of Faraday Electronic Research, Hampton Court. The third was addressed to Hugh Morgan somewhere in Putney. The contents of each envelope was missing. He replaced the envelopes in the order in which he had found them. There were two reasons that he could think of for writing to a dead man. The first was that the girl didn't know that Morgan was dead—the other was that she wanted people to *suppose* that she didn't know. Whichever way it was, it looked as if someone was withholding her mail. He had an odd feeling —like a playwright whose characters came to life, pursuing a plot far beyond the limits of his imagination. The certainty that this girl was not insane grew as he thought about it. And if she was sane, certainly Morgan had been murdered.

He shone his flash along the wall, searching for the door he felt must be there. It was unlocked and gave on a short stretch of corridor linking these offices with the rear of the nursing-home. It was possible for the doctors to reach the observation rooms and wards without having to pass through the entrance hall. He followed the corridor to a smaller hall, dimly lit and, like the passage to the left and stairway in front, covered in sisal matting. The passage connected the front of the building with the kitchens. On each side were numbered rooms—a few of the doors were open. The rest were locked with the keys outside. A quick glance showed these to be empty. He went halfway up the staircase, keeping close to the hall. He peered up into the shadows on the landing above. A faint light glimmered through glass. He guessed at a ward. The doctor's room would surely not be far away. He retraced his steps to the floor below and stood there listening. A woman behind a nearby door moaned in her sleep. He heard movement at the end of the passage. More lights came on. He darted through the first open doorway, feeling for the handle on the inside. There was none. In place of it was a button that operated a spring on contact with the jamb. A last-minute grab prevented it from engaging and locking him inside the room.

He heard a door open, then heels squeaking over the sisal-matting. Only an inch of wood separated them as the nurse passed by, leaving a strong smell of coffee behind her. He heard the tray clatter as she pushed the swing-door, the porter's cantankerous greeting, her sharp retort. Then her footsteps sounded in the hall again. He tracked her by the sound of her feet on the matting, like a wet finger drawn deliberately across glass. It passed and then stopped. He heard her steps retrace. She stopped outside the room where he was hiding.

He retreated behind the slowly opening door till his back was against the wall. Halfway into the room, she paused, near enough for him to have touched her. She swung towards him, one arm outflung as if about to make a speech. A puzzled expression was on her face. She came to life, kicking at his groin as he sprang at her. He jammed his gloved hand against her mouth, too near for her kick to take effect. Their thighs collided. He bore her backwards, collapsing her on the bed. He rammed the pillow over her head, pinning her down with his weight. She tried desperately to defend herself, her legs thrashing ineffectually. He turned her over and sat astride her back. Still holding her down, he used his teeth to rip the sheet lengthways. He tied strips round her ankles and wrists, trussing her like a chicken. He lifted the pillow off her head and gagged her before she could scream. He climbed off the bed and looked down. She stared up at him, her eyes terrified. His own hands were trembling—his heart banging in his rib-cage. The violence of the past few seconds disturbed him deeply. He wanted to say something that would make her understand yet there was nothing he *could* say. He listened in the doorway for the alarm he felt must come. He waited fully a minute but nothing moved. The silent building had assimilated the noise of the struggle without repercussion.

He padded down the passage to the third door on his right and turned the key. He pushed the door open and stepped into the room. He snapped the light on and off, holding it long enough to see the look of startled recognition in the girl's eyes. She was sitting up straight in the bed, her arms stiff beside her. He controlled his voice with difficulty, speaking in a harsh whisper.

"You'll keep your mouth shut if you want to get out of this place alive. Where are your clothes?"

She was a vague huddle against the wall. It was too dark for him to see more than the outline of her face. She imitated his whisper as if they stood on hallowed ground.

"What do you want?"

"Your clothes," he repeated savagely. "Where are they?" He stood over her till she answered.

"I don't know—they took them away."

He brought his face close to hers, speaking as if to an old and well-tried enemy.

"Listen to me. I know you're sane. And I'm the only chance you've got. There's a car outside. I'm ready to drag you into it if I have to. Either that or you come willingly. Which is it going to be?"

She clutched at him. "But you *must* help me. I'll do anything you want."

He caught her wrists. Her entire body was shaking. She was in no shape to climb walls. He had to find an alternative escape route. He gripped her wrists still tighter.

"I owe you nothing—you ought to be the first to admit it. I'll be watching you every inch of the way. Remember that and don't push your luck. Now get out of bed. Whatever I tell you to do, *do* it. Don't ask questions."

He led her down the passage. She followed like a sleepwalker, barefooted under the long nightgown. He pulled her into the end room and let her go. She shrank away as she saw the bound figure on the bed. He undid the knots that tied the nurse to the bedsprings.

"Take her feet."

She nodded, her eyes never leaving his face. They carried the gagged woman along to number 4 and laid her on the bed. He bent low over her, making his voice menacing.

"I'm going to take the gag out of your mouth just long enough to get an answer out of you. Where are this girl's clothes?"

He unfastened the strips in her mouth, his hand ready to silence her. Her voice was completely cowed.

"They're in the cupboards under the stairs. The locks are undone."

He put the gag back in her mouth and covered her up to the eyes with the bedclothes. He jerked his head at the girl and turned the key behind him. They tiptoed along the passage as far as the staircase. The racks in the cupboards were crammed with clothing, each bundle bearing a tag with a name. He searched until he found her clothes and threw them out to her. She hadn't moved but watched him anxiously, clutching the neck of her nightgown.

"Get dressed quickly," he ordered. "There's no time to waste."

She just stood there, showing no sign of obeying him. Her face reddened.

"For Crissakes," he muttered. "You're not in a convent. I'll drag you naked if you make me."

She said nothing—just looked. He went back down the passage saying *Sir Galahad* to himself under his breath. He put his ear against the door of number 4. There was no sound from inside. But sooner or later either the porter or the doctor on duty would miss the nurse and the hunt would be on. He thought of removing the key from the lock but decided against it. She was dressed when he went back to the hall, looking slightly shabby in her two-piece knitwear. She'd made an attempt to put her hair in order but without much success. He pointed at the door behind her. She nodded, obeying him instantly without question, her eyes now like those of a lost animal. He led the way down the connecting passage and into the office where he had found her mail. He shone his flash on the desk, showing her the empty envelopes without saying a word. He was in the act of raising the bottom half of the window when the whiff of shag hit his nostrils. He peered cautiously along the balcony.

The porter was standing at the head of the steps, a flat cap on and smoking a pipe. He was staring into the shadows as though something there had disturbed him.

Duncan stepped back smartly. A clock ticked away on a nearby shelf. Its illuminated hands showed five minutes to eleven. The porter looked set for hours. Duncan imagined the doctor up in his room, the lazy arm stretching out to ring a bell, the man's face when the nurse failed to answer his summons. The steady beat on the shelf persisted. He whirled round as his brain received the message. He crossed the room, guided by the illuminated dial. His fingers cradled the roundness of the alarm clock. He wound the spring, setting the alarm for two minutes to the hour.

He pulled Linda over to the window. They stood shoulder to shoulder, waiting. Suddenly the clock set up a terrific jangle, the unwinding spring sending it skeetering along the shelf. He wrenched up the window as the porter was undoing the door to the outer office. He pushed the girl over the balustrade and dragged her across the courtyard. He undid the wicket-gate and shoved her through. As he closed the small door, lights came on in the room they had just left. The racket of the alarm clock pursued them deep into the trees. Not until they were through the gap Duncan had cut in the barbed wire was it silenced. He pulled the girl to a halt. She stood swaying as he tore at the fastening of the two-way radio set. His breathing came fast.

"Don't waste time talking. Get the car moving. We're coming out by the signpost. Over and out."

They were out of the wood in seconds. The Jaguar whined in the distance. Its driver braked at the signpost and cut his headlamps. The girl lurched forward, stumbling over the rough plough-land. She ran like a panicky hen, arms and legs flailing, head down. Duncan urged her on, his hand in the small of her back. Soft earth was working into his boots so that he seemed to be running on mud soles. He forced a passage through the hawthorn hedge, breaking the branches for her to follow. Chalice had the door open ready for them. He dragged them in as the car started to move.

Crying Eddie gunned the motor. The Jaguar slid fast into the bend behind blinking headlamps. Linda and Duncan sat squashed together in the narrow space at the back.

The speedometer needle crept up into the eighties. Crying Eddie's voice was as nonchalant as his touch of the wheel.

"There's a crossroad coming up in about three minutes. Do you want me to go left, right or straight on?"

The rear end of the car snaked out of the curve, sending the girl swinging against Duncan. She stayed there with rigid body till he pushed her upright again. The radio crackled incessantly. Chalice lit a cigarette with a steady hand. He sounded pleased with himself.

"We're tuned in on the police-band. If there's any action, we'll hear it. You want to double that bet, Crying?"

Crying Eddie aimed the headlamps between rushing hedges. "The crossroad's coming up in about one minute now. Make your minds up."

Chalice turned his head round facing the pair in the back. "You're the boss, Ritchie. Tell him."

Duncan started ridding himself of the things stuffed in his clothing. He dumped the canvas roll and radio set on the floor.

"Just get us to any station on the main line—any station that serves trains to London. I've left a nurse behind gagged and tied. I don't know how long it's going to be before they find her. If there *is* a chase. I don't want you guys involved."

Chalice put an end to his partner's ironical humming. "*Think*, Crying—unless you want your collar felt. A main-line station somewhere near here."

The answer came with the speed and authority of a computing machine.

"Reading. There are trains up to London every half-hour or so. We can make it there in a little over that."

"Reading it is." Chalice rummaged under the seat. He tossed a woman's mac and a package of Kleenex back into the girl's lap. "You'd better clean some of that dirt off your feet and legs. Haven't you got anything to put over your hair?"

She shook her head. Chalice pulled the silk square from his shirt-neck. He gave it to her, untied his shoes and handed them back to Duncan. He added a reversible driving-coat that he picked from the seat next to him.

"Put these shoes on. Crying's coat will hide the worst of those tears in your trousers. And see she keeps that mac on, Ritchie. Make her keep the scarf round her nut. One last thing—we'll drive you to London if you want it—you know that."

They were travelling through villages already asleep. The speedometer needle rarely dropped below sixty. Crying Eddie's voice was like a train announcer's.

"We'll be coming into Reading in another ten minutes."

Duncan finished tying his shoelaces. The girl had already bound her hair in Chalice's scarf, tying it French-fashion. With the white mac, it completely altered her appearance. He tapped her on the knee.

"You can see what's happening. People are sticking their necks out for you as well as for me. How are you going to play this?"

She turned a blank face towards him, her face uncertain. "Play it—I don't understand you."

He had the feeling that three people were waiting for his answer.

"I'm going to make you talk," he said steadily. "And if you think that's tough, I have some news for you. Your boy-friend's dead."

There was just light enough in the back of the car to see her eyes, dark pools in a wedge of pallor.

"You're lying," she whispered.

"I don't have to lie," he answered. "Dead and buried—fished out of the river. And you're next on the list. You can talk to the cops about it when I've finished with you if you like but first you're going to talk to me."

Her head sagged between her shoulders. Chalice seemed about to touch her. Duncan pushed his hand away.

"Keep out of this, Harry. This is between her and me."

They were cruising under sodium arcs through the out-

133

skirts of Reading. There were people still on the streets—traffic—the lights of the city centre showed ahead. Linda still sagged, half-supported by Duncan's shoulder. Suddenly she sat up, her face completely expressionless. She dabbed at wet cheeks with the back of a hand.

"I don't know," she said. "I just don't know any more."

"That's a right giggle, isn't it?" Crying Eddie observed before Chalice silenced him.

"There's only one thing you *can* do," urged Duncan. "Run for cover—get yourself out of this jam and take me with you. I'm not a liar, Linda. I'll help you."

She shivered and then answered. "I'll do whatever you say."

He touched her leg briefly and spoke to the driver. "Drop us off at the station."

Chalice's shoulders lifted. "It's your party, mate. We'll be home before you are. Give us a blow as soon as you get into Paddington. And take it easy. I've got a bet with Dasher here at the wheel. I think he's getting worried. And I don't get his fiver till she's safe in the flat."

Midnight was up on the station clock as Duncan and the girl passed through the barrier. The indicator-board warned of a quarter-hour wait for the next London train. He took her arm, steering her to a bench at the far end of the track. They sat down. He put himself between her and the exit. The other passengers near them looked harmless enough. A pair of lovers, a couple of middle-aged women busy with banalities, a haggard man carrying a violin case.

Duncan tightened his grip on the girl's arm as he felt her move. She turned her head towards him slowly, staring at him in a sort of wonder.

"You're hurting me. I'm not going to run away."

The man with the violin-case walked by, his eyes sliding sideways as he passed. She searched Duncan's face anxiously.

"Where would I go?" she asked.

He relaxed his grip cautiously. Somehow she managed to make the problem sound as much his as hers and he resented it.

"Don't waste your time playing for me," he said sarcastically. "I'm immune. You've got nothing I want except some good answers and I don't expect to get those in bed."

She averted her head and shrugged. "Will you tell me your name?" she said after a while.

"Sure," he said equably. "Ritchie Duncan. The barman at the *Cintra*, remember? The guy you stuck with that film."

She opened swollen lids on eyes heavy with tears. "You're not being fair, Mr. Duncan. Shall I tell you something—I've never *had* anything anyone wanted. Don't you find that odd?"

She did it well, the small lost voice and tears—the faint surprise at a cruel world. He resented her touting the act to him of all people.

"Don't you *know* what you've done to me?" he exploded. "What do you take me for—some back-street bum feeling his oats? I've seen you six times in my life. You walk into a bar and ask a favour. Next thing that happens my job's gone, people try to break my back and you tell me you've never had anything anyone wanted! Do you suppose I *care*? Not a word of excuse or apology, just you and your bleeding heart. I'll tell you exactly who I am, Miss Swann. I'm an ex-con—a man with a police-record. Nobody wants what *I've* got either and all they need is the chance to prove it. But this time they're wrong and what's more *you're* going to tell them that they're wrong."

A freight train rattled by. She let the last box-car go before she answered.

"Is Hugh really dead? You must tell me—it's important."

He lit a cigarette with tremulous fingers, brooding over the flame, his mind with the speeding Jaguar. Chalice's liberty was not risked lightly. But once the pledge was made it was fulfilled. The irony of it all was pointed. His only source of help came from the world whose values he had rejected. He fashioned his phrases for each to be deliberately destructive.

"Sure he's dead with a coroner's verdict to prove it. You were right enough—there's no hole left for you to crawl into

—no shoulder left to cry on. Just me. And I'm about as cuddlesome as a rattlesnake."

She swayed, pitching forward to the ground before he could catch her. He turned towards the two women bustling in his direction. He bent over the girl's prostrate body, speaking hurriedly.

"Get up!"

She was lying on her side, an arm outflung. One of the women threw her handbag on the bench and knelt by the girl. She unfastened Linda's clothing, rapping Duncan with her tongue.

"Sitting there doing nothing—can't you see the girl's fainted?"

He pushed her aside and took her place. Linda's forehead and cheeks were heavy with sweat, her hands cold. He lifted them in his own. Her pulse was strong but erratic. He raised her to the bench, vaguely aware that someone was offering a flask. He forced the liquid through her clenched teeth. She struggled up, staring round the gathered ring of faces. Her eyes unfogged and she shoved the woman's hand away. She grabbed Duncan's arm.

"I'm all right now, thank you," she said slowly. "My husband will take care of me."

He got her on her feet. They walked to the end of the track, she leaning on him heavily. The public-address system announced the imminent arrival of the London train. A locomotive hooted in the near darkness. He gave her his handkerchief. She wiped her neck and brow and lowered her head between her knees. He wanted to touch her, betrayed by a sense of pity. She could have walked away from him back there—claimed protection from anyone in the crowd. The truth was that she *had* no place to go—any more than he did.

She lifted her head, speaking as if she could read his thoughts.

"That was silly of me—it won't happen again. I want to help you, Mr. Duncan. I suppose I'm the only one who really can."

The train hissed to a halt. He found an empty first-class compartment and pulled the blinds down. She took the scarf off her head and put it in her lap.

"He said I had to wear it but I feel so hot."

He found himself looking at her critically for the first time. Her head was like that on an Irish bank-note. Long, sad and haunting, with wild reddish hair. He bundled his coat into a pillow for her.

"Time enough when we get to Paddington. Meanwhile put your feet up and try to rest."

He cut the light and sat in darkness relieved only by a small blue lamp in the ceiling. A new sense of responsibility disturbed him. She slept—or seemed to sleep—not stirring till the train rumbled through Westbourne Grove. Then she sat up, blinking as he switched on the lights. She cleared a patch on the steamed window, making a face at her reflection. She looked at him with a faint smile.

"We forgot my bag. I don't even have a lipstick."

He donned Crying Eddie's coat and gave her his comb. "You'll do—we're getting straight into a cab. How do you feel?"

She stopped in the middle of retying the scarf round her head, watching him as if his reaction mattered.

"Terrible."

He nodded. "I'm past it. I've been thinking while you were asleep. Maybe I *am* wrong about you. Did you know what was in that envelope when you pushed it over the bar?"

She nodded her head slowly. "Yes. But that's only part of it—you see . . ."

He broke in impatiently. "We'll talk later. I just want to know one thing now, Linda. Who took you to that asylum?"

Her eyes were suddenly fearful. Her mouth twisted with effort.

"One of the doctors was there and I was in an ambulance." She hid her face in her arms as if he had struck her.

He reached across and freed them gently. "Forget it. You got me into this, now I'm the one who's got to finish it. There is no other way. I'm taking you to friends—maybe not your kind of friends but you'll be safe there, I promise you. In the morning we'll talk. Now lift your head—that's it. What do you say?"

She stared at him for a long time before she replied. "I'll go wherever you say. And whatever you tell me, I'll do. I give you my word on that, Mr. Duncan.

He smiled wryly. "Ritchie. I guess we know one another well enough for that."

The train was stopping. He lowered the window and looked out along the track. It was almost empty. A few baggage porters were trundling trolleys towards the first-class compartment. Steel wheels combined with steam and buffers in a cacophony that echoed through the glass-domed terminus. The raw night air smelled of tunnels and oil vapour. He opened the door, jumped out and gave her a hand.

"Just try to look as though you did this every night of your life. If anyone stops us, I'll do the talking."

They passed through the barrier, anonymous in the crowd. He steered her to the phone booth and called Chalice's number. The enclosed space forced their bodies into intimacy. She neither shrank from nor encouraged the contact, the warmth of her leg firm against his. He listened to the dialling tone, watching the scene outside for the danger he feared. People dozed on the benches in the great hall, surrounded by their baggage. A couple of negroes dressed in flamboyant suits eyed the passing women. A few yards away a youth with filthy clothing was combing shoulder-length hair with his fingers. Doting on him was a pregnant teenager in trousers. Hard-eyed military policemen and railroad cops prowled through the benches, hunting their prey in pairs.

Chalice's voice was laconic. "It's all sweet this end. Take a cab as far as Grove Road. I make it about twenty-five to one. At one o'clock I'll send the night-porter out for some cigarettes. There'll be nobody downstairs in the hall—one o'clock on the dot, remember."

Duncan replaced the receiver. "Everything's o k. They're waiting for us."

He flagged a cab on the corner of Praed Street. It was five to one as he paid off the driver. They started walking slowly up Grove Road in the direction of Chalice's apartment building. As they neared the lighted entrance, a uniformed porter scuttled by, going the other way. The soft-carpeted hall absorbed the sound of their footsteps. Duncan thumbed the elevator button. The penthouse door was ajar. He pushed her into the hall. She stood, looking into the mirror, freed her hair and then shrugged.

"They're friends," he reassured her. "In you go."

The living-room curtains were drawn, the space-heated air stuffy with the smell of Chalice's cigar. He was sitting on the sofa with Crying Eddie. He lifted a hand in salute.

"The favourite home and dried—that's the way I like to see them run, Crying! Pour the young lady a drink. What'll it be, dear—scotch, gin, champagne—you name it and we've got it. Don't be nervous—we're all pals here."

The parrot had been uncovered. It shuffled the length of its chain chanting obscenities. Duncan pulled a chair for Linda. She sat down, looking at him for guidance. He touched her shoulder.

"A brandy'll do you good. Then you go to bed."

Chalice yawned. "We'll *all* go to bed. I need some kip— I'm not used to this excitement. The porter'll be back with the cigarettes, Crying. Give him a dollar on your way out."

Crying Eddie unwound his legs, gave the girl a brief inspection, then dismissed her.

"You and your dollars," he said sourly. "I could retire on the loot I have to lay out for you. 'Give the cigarette-girl a couple of quid, Crying!'—'Don't forget to take care of the guy on the door!' What's the matter—you given up carrying money?"

Chalice grinned. "I know you like to be the big spender. You owe me a fiver anyway on the bet—take it off the bill. And give him his coat back for Gawd's sake, Ritchie—it's his big flash with all these kinky birds he gets hold of. He tells them he's a racing-driver, don't you, Crying?"

His partner took his time doing up his buttons. "I don't tell 'em I've written books about my experiences in the army. The army," he repeated with extreme distaste. "The only time you was out of the glasshouse was when you were on the run. Hero. I'll call you in the morning. Goodnight, Ritchie—goodnight, dear—you're in real dangerous company."

Chalice waited till the front door had closed. He sighed and stubbed out his cigar. "That Crying—always exaggerating. They'd have been in dead trouble in Korea if it hadn't been for me." He leaned back, handsome and confident, smiling at the girl. He opened and shut an eye. "Jealous—that's what they are, dear."

She looked at him uncomprehendingly, then drained the glass of brandy. Her voice was jerky. She spoke as if their understanding were important to her.

"I didn't mean what I said on the station. *He* wanted me. We were going to be married, you know. That's why he did it."

Chalice glanced at Duncan and shrugged. The Canadian took the empty glass from her limp fingers.

"Come on," he said quietly. "Bed for you." He showed her the room, drew the curtains and switched on the heater. He turned the lights on in the adjoining bathroom. The mirror reflected an array of bottles on the jade-green makeup table.

"You'll find everything you want there—use it. The key's on the inside of your door. We'll talk in the morning. Goodnight, Linda."

She looked at the turned-back bedclothes, the clean pyjamas on the pillow and swivelled slowly. She touched his cheek with the very tips of her fingers. She took a deep breath.

"I don't know why but I don't think I'll ever forget you. Whatever happens, I'll never forget you. Goodnight, Ritchie."

She shut the door quietly behind him, leaving the key unturned. Chalice was teasing the parrot with an empty cigarette-pack. He looked at Duncan quizzically.

"I don't know what you're thinking, mate, but I hope it's the same as what I am."

Duncan half-filled a glass with scotch. Chalice had turned the sofa into a bed while he'd been out of the room. He sat on the end of it, swishing the ice cubes round in his glass.

"What *are* you thinking, Harry?" he asked quietly.

A hint of embarrassment showed in Chalice's face. He looked away.

"Bugger off, Ritchie," he said in a level voice. "Now— tonight. I'll take care of everything. That bird means more trouble, I can smell it a mile off. You've made your point— she's out—now drop her. I've got an idea for you. Phil Daniels is in Zürich, I can send you to him. He's your kind of thief—he could probably put something your way."

Duncan put his glass down. The scotch was doing nothing for him—he might as well have been drinking water.

"I told you, Harry, I quit. I meant it. You say you'd take care of things. What happens to the girl, for instance?"

Chalice shifted his stance. "She lives happily ever after, mate, that's what. What do you care—she's a menace—a nut on the run. She'll get you crucified, Ritchie."

Duncan nodded. "Sure—that's exactly what you're supposed to believe. That's why they stuck her in that place— nobody's going to listen to the ramblings of a head-case."

Chalice glanced at the ceiling. His voice was disbelieving. "Are the doctors supposed to be villains too, then?"

Duncan brushed by him and went to the bookcase. He ran a hand along the shelves, searching for the volume he wanted. He pulled it out, standing stockstill as he saw the .32 calibre automatic hidden behind it. He turned and faced Chalice. Both men looked at one another without a word being said. Finally Duncan shrugged. He started to read from the book he was holding.

" 'Law for the Layman.' Your bible—now listen to this. 'Mental Health Act, 1959' '. . . an application for admission

141

for treatment shall be founded on the written recommendation of two medical practitioners . . .' blah, blah, blah. '. . . on the grounds that the patient is suffering from mental disorder' etc. There's a hell of a lot more to it than that but the facts are simple. Two doctors can put you inside—you, me, anyone. All it needs is for one of them to be crooked. Maybe he has a big reputation, Harry. People respect his opinion. It follows, doesn't it, that the other doctor's going to be halfway convinced long before he even sees the patient. Why is he going to admit to an opinion that differs from the big man's? What's so fantastic about this? You were innocent but the law still put you away, didn't it?"

Chalice took the book from Duncan's grasp—read a few pages and returned it to its place on the shelf. He did not touch the gun. When he turned round, his expression was unconvinced.

"You want to know what I think, Ritchie—I think you've got too much imagination. Crooked doctors—industrial spies! What I want to know is what do they get from her—why should she be so important? Don't tell me it's for that lousy bit of film Crying Eddie collected!"

Duncan lowered his voice. There must be no mistake about his intention. He was going on, alone if he had to.

"The film, Harry, that's right. The lousy bit of film. One man's dead because of it. I've told you what they tried to do to me. Don't talk about imagination, chum. It's a different game! that's all. You don't want to admit that it exists because you don't know the rules. Goodnight, Harry. I'll be pulling out in the morning."

Chalice pivoted with his right arm drawn back. He grinned shamefacedly and lowered it.

"And you know the rules, is that it, Ritchie?"

Duncan lowered a blocking hand. The moment let in a flood of memories—of three men cooped in a cell designed for one—of tempers fine-drawn with frustration. He'd faced Chalice a dozen times in this way—ready for violence that never came. Then as now, something had always brought the pair of them to their senses.

"I don't know them, no, Harry," he said in a quiet voice. "But I intend to learn. I've *got* to learn. The girl says she's going to help me—we'll see."

Chalice hooded the bird and yawned. "O k, o k. I've said my piece. You want to be a gang-buster, that's your business. Me and Crying'll come along for the laughs. I put your toothbrush in the kitchen. I'll have to phone down and leave a message for the old bag who does my cleaning. We don't want her up here in the morning. It's been a fair old night, Ritchie—let's get some kip."

Duncan draped his sweater on a chair. The other man talked as if everything that had happened had been part of some gigantic practical joke. There was still something to be said—he did it the best way he knew how.

"You've had your say, Harry, now let me have mine. I know the way you feel about people expressing gratitude —you mistrust it. I don't know whether or not I'd have done as much for you—I like to think I would but I can't be sure. I guess the truth is that a guy can't turn legitimate and feel the same way about things. But whatever happens, Harry, I want you to remember this—I'm grateful."

Chalice turned back in his doorway. "That's all right, mate. My advice to you is to go back where you belong once this is all over. Don't be like some of these hooks who go respectable and then creep back after dark—when they can't be seen—trying to chat-up their old pals. It don't work, mate. As far as I'm concerned you'll be a dead member and good luck to you."

"A dead member—that's about as low as you can go in your book, isn't it, Harry?"

Chalice smiled and his smile was utterly friendly. "Just about, mate. But don't let it worry you. Goodnight, Ritchie."

The overheated room stank of Chalice's cigar smoke. Duncan flung the windows wide and stretched out on the sofa. He fell asleep listening to the parrot's meaningless croaking.

143

Linda Swann

She woke without sense of time, knowing only that she'd slept long and heavily. She sat up, looking round the unfamiliar room. It was decorated in a strange way as if by a night-club hostess with religion. A chain of autographed champagne corks hung from the dressing-table mirror. There were a couple of signed pictures of filmstars, a large silver cross and a tangle of rosaries. A missal lay side by side with a copy of *Fanny Hill* on the bedside table. The open clothes closet showed an apparently endless array of coats and dresses. She threw back the covers and went to the window. The apartment was ten storeys up. It seemed a long way down to the hoop of asphalt where parked cars glistened with winter rime. Quiet decorous houses faced the apartment building. She watched a roadsweeper chase a flurry of leaves along the gutter. It all looked very peaceful and yet she turned away from the window with a strong sense of foreboding.

She used the green bathroom, taking advantage of the well-stocked cosmetic shelf. Her stockings were badly laddered. She searched drawers till she found what must have been a hundred pairs of new nylons, carelessly stuffed on top of one another. She pulled on a pair under the wide-eyed stare of the girl in the picture on the wall. Lifesize, it represented a goodlooking teenager in a bikini lolling on hot sand in strong sunshine.

Linda opened her bedroom door. A radio was playing somewhere in the kitchen. She smelled toast and coffee. The living-room was empty. Someone had done a rough cleaning job on it. The ash-trays had been emptied, the parrot's perch placed by the window. Sheets and blankets were piled neatly on the end of the velvet sofa. She swung round as the kitchen door opened.

Duncan carried the tray to the table and nodded. "Hi! I don't have to ask you how you slept. I took a look at you about half-past nine and thought you were dead. There's toast here and marmalade—I don't know what you normally eat for breakfast. It's a meal I usually skip. If you want more food the kitchen's full of it. Do you take cream with your coffee?"

She smiled her thanks and took the rough earthenware bowl in her hands. He was sitting on the sofa, inspecting her in a way that was somehow flattering. She dropped her eyes, feeling her cheeks and neck redden. He looked older and harder and, for reasons that she didn't try to analyse, physically attractive. He was wearing a pair of slacks and a fine wool shirt that clung to a good pair of shoulders. He had nicked himself shaving, the tiny shred of cotton that staunched the bleeding white against his faintly tanned cheeks. He lit a couple of cigarettes and gave her one. From him the gesture was unaffected.

"There's nobody here but you and me, Linda. And we've got to talk. You must tell me everything—you know why, don't you?"

"Yes," she said slowly. "Yes I know why. Where must I start?"

"At the beginning," he said impatiently. "And leave nothing out."

She looked away, disturbed by his change in manner. Lying in the darkened train she had wanted to confide in him—to rid herself of some of the pent-up fear and misery of the last days. But he seemed to have altered overnight. As if his sympathy and kindness were once more suspended. Her hands began to shake. She hid them behind her back, struggling to produce words that her lips refused.

He inhaled deeply. She knew by the way he blew out the smoke that he was trying to control himself.

"Now look, Linda," he said. "This is something we've got to get out of our systems. I can't tell your story—I can only listen. You and Morgan worked together—one of you had

145

the idea that Faraday's trade-secrets would be worth money. Or did somebody outside put up the proposition?"

His voice gave her the courage she needed. She huddled in a cloud of nervously-blown smoke, remembering aloud. He listened to her in silence, lighting one cigarette after another, watching her face carefully. She only faltered once, the sound of Hugh's bitter contempt a knife in her memory. Finally she was done. She drank her coffee not caring that it was lukewarm.

Duncan crossed to the window and stood looking out, his back to her.

"You still believe in the guy Morgan, don't you?"

She turned the question over in her mind. Hugh was dead but once he had loved her. That she believed and she had to say so.

"You don't understand. There was so much in life that Hugh hadn't had. He grew up in the slums—he was practically self-educated. Instead of being proud of it he hated everything that reminded him of those days. And there were so many things that did. Me perhaps most of all. He despised everything he thought I stood for, really. The sad thing is that at the end I failed him—not vice-versa."

He turned to face her. He shook his head. "Haven't you had enough heart-aches without saddling yourself with more? I want to know one thing. I still need you, Linda. And I think you owe me your help. Will you fail *me*?"

Her denial was swift and vehement. "You know I won't. I told you so last night. I don't matter any more—I don't really care what happens to me. But I do care about putting things right."

He came across the room and took her face in his hands. She looked into troubled eyes and offered her lips soundlessly. He merely touched her shoulder.

"It'll work out, Linda. I can't be sure how but I promise it'll all work out. Tell me something—did anyone apart from Morgan ever mention money to you—a sum?"

"Just Hugh. He said they were going to give him ten thousand pounds for the film."

He dragged a chair close to her. "Listen to me—I've got a telephone number that two of these guys left at the house where I was living. I want you to ring this number—tell them who you are and say that the film is in your possession. You must say that you'll only part with it when you're sure of the money. Do you think you can handle that, Linda?"

She struggled with reborn fear. "But they're murderers. They know I'd never go near them again. They're bound to suspect things from the start."

His eyes narrowed and brightened. "Let me worry about that. Do you know what happens on a tiger-hunt, Linda? They stake-out an animal and sit in the trees and wait. The tiger's so busy watching the lure that he forgets about the hunters."

Her voice faltered. "And I'm the lure?"

His hand swung in a gesture of denial. "You won't even go near the place. I want an address, Linda. The address they'll expect you to come to. And long before you're supposed to arrive, I'll be there. I'm going to flush these bastards out into the open."

He opened a drawer in the desk and gave her a handful of glossy prints.

"Read them a couple of those headings if they sound at all reluctant. Wait till I get on the extension and then dial."

She watched him into Chalice's bedroom. He left the two doors wide open. He sat on the bed, took the phone off the stand and nodded at her. She spelled out the number he had given her. The buzzer sounded, insistent and ominous. Then a voice answered.

"Flaxman 9872."

"You know who I am," she said carefully. "I have something that you want."

She could hear something ticking through the sudden silence.

"I see," the voice answered slowly. "Where are you?"

"I have what you want," she repeated. "But the price has gone up. I want fifteen thousand pounds."

She had the impression that a hand was covering the mouthpiece at the other end of the line.

The voice continued. "You might be bluffing. You have a reputation for it."

She read a line of print at the top of one of the photographs. "There are seven more—do you want me to read them?"

The voice sharpened. "No. It's essential that you keep off the streets, you realize that. You know that the police are looking for you?"

Her mouth had completely dried. She glanced through the open doorways. Duncan's face contorted. She realized that he wanted her to answer.

"I understand," she said.

"Then listen carefully. Take a taxi to number two Elleston Place—that's off Oakley Street, Chelsea. You'll see a pub on the corner. Number two is almost opposite—a house with a green door. Be there at four o'clock. Have you any money?"

She looked again for guidance. Duncan nodded. "Yes." she said. "I have that. Number two Elleston Place. You understand that I won't be bringing the articles with me—or possibly only part of them to prove that I mean business. I shall expect a down payment on the sum mentioned—is that clear?"

The answer followed the same muffled pause. "Four o'clock then and keep off the streets." The line went dead.

Duncan stood in the doorway holding up both thumbs at her. He moved with speed and decision. He pulled a set of survey-maps from the bookcase and spread one across the carpet.

"You were great. I think he's probably right about the police looking for you but you're safe enough here. Let's take a look at number two Elleston Place."

He knelt on the floor close to her, tracing a course on the map. His finger drew a small circle.

"Here we are. You see this little cross—that means a church. This must be a graveyard behind it. I reckon it no more than thirty yards from the house. I can track a fly across the front window with a good pair of binoculars."

He folded the map and took it over to the bookshelves. As he pushed it into place a dislodged book fell to the ground. He masked the gap in the shelf hurriedly with his body. His manner was almost too casual.

"That's it, Linda. I've got to leave you now. Bolt the door top and bottom after me. I'll be back about six. I'll push a box of matches through the mail-box so that you'll know who it is. No matter who else rings *don't open the door*! The same goes for the phone. If it's me, it'll ring twice and then stop. It'll do that three times. Only pick up the receiver *then*—otherwise leave it strictly alone."

She moved her head in assent. "Couldn't I come with you?" she asked hesitantly. "I'd feel safer."

He belted his coat and slung a binocular-case festooned with race badges over one arm.

"You're safe here. It's possible that the cops may be looking for me—we can be fairly certain that they're looking for you. The moment you put your nose outside this door you're on your way back to Brierley. And if ever that happens, you're strictly on your own. I wouldn't know where to start."

He said the last few words with a sort of hopelessness that shamed her.

She smiled at him and followed him into the hall.

"I'll be all right," she promised.

He shot the two bolts, explaining the mechanism with a smile.

"They're burglar-proof. If you get bored, start putting your story on paper. Sooner or later you're going to need it."

The idea both shocked and puzzled her. "What on earth for?"

He looked at her oddly. "Because life never works out as we expect it to, Linda. I'm going to settle with these people my own way. But when the shouting dies down, you'll have to do some settling of your own. With the Faraday people.

They'll prosecute you for theft—they must. Whatever I can do I'll do but this is something you've got to accept."

The mirror behind him reflected a face that she suddenly loathed. Every defeated pretence in her life seemed to be written on it—each useless quest for protection that ended up by alienating the protector.

"I accept everything," she said. "You needn't worry about that. Good luck and be careful."

He undid the door and waved from the elevator gates. She watched him along the road from the living-room window. As soon as he had turned the corner, she ran to the book-shelves and pulled out the red-covered book. He had been quick, putting himself in front of what was behind but not quick enough to prevent her from seeing the automatic pistol. She carried it to the sofa, handling a gun for the first time in her life with a mixture of relief and revulsion.

A tiny button on the stock moved between two dots. She set it so that the red one was left exposed. She lifted the barrel and placed it against her forehead. The pressure was cold and hard on her temple. The mechanics of suicide were simple. One jerk on the trigger and everything that people had always expected of her would be fulfilled. She lowered her hand, amazed at its steadiness. It was easy and there'd be no prosecution, no disgrace, just oblivion.

She swung sharply towards the parrot as it squawked a bar-room insult at her. She covered its head with the cloth and started walking aimlessly round the room. She was posing again—she didn't even have the courage to rid herself of her misery. Her cowardice gave her a deep sense of guilt. She stopped at the desk, looking down at the drawer. She pulled it open on impulse. The film and the folder of prints were fastened together with an elastic band. She snatched them up in her hand, looking about her as if Duncan were still in the apartment. She stared down, the gun in one hand, the film in the other. He'd called himself a crook—a man with a criminal record—driving the words home like nails, to punish and wound. Yet he'd given her in that brief time more understanding than she had ever had before. And she would drain it dry—just as she'd drained every source of sympathy before it. *Life never works out as we expect it to* . . . But it could. She would *make* it work for him. Those men had already tried to kill him. Unless they got what they wanted they would try again. She put the film back in the drawer and shut it. She knew now what she must do. As long as the film stayed in her possession she could set the terms for its surrender. She would ask for no money—nothing except Duncan's safety. If she succeeded, the long list of failures in her life wouldn't really matter.

She found an empty handbag in the clothes-closet. The .32 pistol fitted into it unobtrusively. She filled her pocket with sixpences filched from a pinch-bottle that was full of them. She picked up the telephone and dialled the Chelsea number. The same voice answered immediately.

She spoke in a rush. "There's a change in plans. I have to come now. I'm leaving right away."

She hung up without waiting for an answer. She left the apartment, shutting the door after her with a feeling of finality. She had no means of returning. The porter on duty in the hall looked at her curiously.

"A taxi, miss? I'll ring for one right away."

She took a seat on a brocade sofa. The face in the fake Louis XV mirror was dark-eyed with a mouth boldly slashed with unfamiliar red. But it wasn't a frightened face, she told herself. Nor one that she hated any more. She looked up, realizing that the porter was speaking to her.

"I asked what direction you're going in, miss. They want to know."

She smiled at him. "Oh, of course. Chelsea. And will you tell him to hurry, please."

She walked from the bottom of Oakley Street. The corner pub was open. She used some of her dwindling stock of coins to buy herself a drink and carried her glass to a table by the window. The church and graveyard Duncan had indicated were on her left. Number two Elleston Place was diagonally across the street. She wondered who would be waiting for her behind the green-painted door. They might even be in the pub—doing as she was—using it as a place from which to reconnoitre.

She put her drink down hastily and looked round the bar. A pale-haired man standing in front of the fire straightened his tie self-consciously and smiled. A group of beards and sweaters were making a loud knowledgeable chatter about the expertise involved in television writing. Their females, chalk-faced and long-booted, listened indifferently. The weight in her handbag was suddenly reassuring. They would be expecting a frightened woman and they would be wrong. She wasn't even frightened of the police. She had passed two constables at the end of the bridge. Their interest in her hadn't gone further than her legs.

She studied the front of the house. The windows were blank and curtained. Empty milk bottles stood on the top step. A dank unswept slope led down to a garage. She left the drink and the bar, loitering long enough in the passage to make sure that she had not been followed. She crossed the street and climbed the steps. A handful of pamphlets protruded through the mail-flap. She raised the heavy knocker. The clatter it made echoed through the house without evoking response. She looked over her shoulder, half-expecting someone to call her from the street or the garage below. Her eye caught movement behind the window on her left. The door opened. She wrapped the handle of the handbag round her wrist and walked in. She heard the bolts being shot home and smelled garlic. Fingers touched her sleeve. She recognized the voice on the phone.

"Straight through—the door on your right."

The back room was curtained like the others, lit by a standard lamp in the corner. Except for a desk, the furniture was covered with dust-sheets. The desk appeared to have been ransacked. Paper ash was thick in the firegrate. Lying on the carpet was a stuffed ant-eater. Ashe bent down and lifted it into position. He slumped indifferently on the shrouded sofa, roundfaced and ruddy. The ragged scar was livid through his thin hair. He extended a gloved hand toward her. She aimed the barrel squarely at his stomach.

"Don't touch me—don't any of you ever touch me again! If you're expecting the film I've brought nothing with me except this." She moved the gun a fraction.

He sat quite still, his eyes moving like those of a farmer bidding at a cattle-auction. He placed a hand on each knee, the movements slow and deliberate.

"I advise you to shut the door to the hall, Miss Swann. This house is supposed to be empty. It's important to us both that the neighbours continue to think so."

She leaned back against the closed door, certain that he respected the gun. He just wanted her to think that he wasn't afraid.

"You can have the film," she said suddenly. "Not for money but in return for Duncan's safety."

He tilted his head. "You're a little late for that sort of bargain. You see, we're no longer interested in the film."

She watched his expression closely, disbelieving him. "Then why did you bring me here?"

He shrugged. "To offer you a different kind of bargain. A chance to build a better world. I underestimated you, Miss Swann. Seriously."

She looked at him dumbfounded. "A better world did you say? You must be insane. You've killed Hugh—with me you were even crueller. Yes, you're insane, all of you. Do you know what I'm going to do—I'm going to the police and you're coming with me."

He turned his hands over, offering them cupped as a beggar might have done.

"That was a very stupid thing for you to have said. Now you won't leave this house alive. Surely you didn't think that I was here alone—look!"

She shook her head, refusing to be caught. She tightened her finger on the trigger till the resistance was taut.

"Get on your feet," she said.

He obeyed, standing with his head bowed on powerful shoulders. Suddenly his foot flashed out, dragging a length of flex in its train. The standard-lamp toppled sideways. A flash lit the darkness as the gun jumped in her hand. Her ears rang with pain, then his whole weight hit her breast-high. He fell on top of her, his powerful fingers seeking her neck arteries. Her legs thrashed violently but after a while she lay still.

Ritchie Duncan

HE sat on the rented motor-cycle, crash-helmeted and goggled. Number two Elleston Place was just visible through the railings of the tiny park. A buzzer sounded in the bar across the way, chasing the last customers from the pub on the corner. It was half-past two—an hour-and-a-half before Linda was expected in the house with the green-painted door. He put a chain through the back wheel of the motor-cycle, padlocked it and walked up Elleston Place. As he passed number two, he glanced up the steps casually, certain that he was completely unrecognizable. The house looked dirty and deserted, its drawn curtains and empty milk-bottles an invitation to the first boy-burglar who happened along the street. This meant absolutely nothing. They might well use an apparently empty house as a base.

The wall of the churchyard ran north for about fifty yards—from the pub lavatories to the church itself. He took off his goggles, loitering in front of stained parochial notices displayed on a mildewed board. There was no one on the street. He climbed a couple of steps and tried the latch of the nail-studded door. It lifted easily. He stepped into the church quickly and shut the door behind him. The interior smelled of beeswax. Bronze chrysanthemums flanked a simple cross on the altar. The candles were unlit. He took off his helmet and sat in a back pew. Stained-glass filtered the light to semi-obscurity. He sat with his head pillowed in his arms in an attitude of prayer, listening. The only sound was the tapping of a blind-cord against the window.

He picked his way over the hassocks to a side-door leading from the nave to the churchyard. It was locked on the inside. He unfastened it. Ivy rambled over the wall dividing the street from the churchyard, wreathing forgotten headstones. Little sun touched the graveyard. The grass was lank and pallid, the granite and marble upholstered in velvet fungus. The only tree was an old yew at the far end. He walked towards it, affecting an interest in the memorial stones. Once under its branches, he looked up at the windows showing over the wall. There was no indication that he was being watched. A quick scramble took him into the lower half of the tree. He went on up till he was on a level well above the top of the wall. He unslung the binoculars and stretched out, supporting his body with splayed legs. The bark and foliage gave off an acidulous odour that irritated his nostrils.

He turned the small wheel bringing the façade of number two into sharp focus. The powerful lens brought him close to the curtained windows, the mail-box stuffed with circulars. A steep slope made it impossible for anyone to use the roof as a means of escape. No smoke rose from the chimneys. He trained the glasses on the ramp leading down to the garage doors. Tyre tracks showed in a patch of mud at the bottom—whether new or old it was difficult to judge. The house looked as though it might have been abandoned for weeks or even months. He settled into a more comfortable position, watching the street both ways from the green-painted door. It was gone four when a cab slowed, coming from the Embankment. The driver was obviously searching for a number. Duncan raised the glasses only to lower them as the cab continued on its way. It stopped half-a-dozen houses higher. Another quarter-of-an-hour passed. Lights came on in the street. He checked his watch. It was well after five—way past the time of Linda's rendezvous. He'd been there nearly three hours and learnt exactly nothing. He dropped out of the tree and brushed the mould from his overalls. Lights had come on inside the church as well. He ran in the shadow of the wall to the side door. He opened it with infinite care. The nave was empty but someone was moving about out of sight up in the organ loft. He slipped through, closing the door as the organist started his voluntary. He tiptoed from one pillar to the next and let himself out to the street. Number two was the only house without lights.

He walked as far as the telephone booths at the north end of the Albert Bridge. Chalice would be waiting at the club. He half-dialled the number and stopped, impelled by a sense of misgiving. He rang the penthouse instead, using the agreed signal. The phone continued to ring unanswered. He spent five minutes at it, telling himself that she was sleeping—in the bath—anything rather than accept the truth he was beginning to fear. There was still no response. Chalice himself answered the call to the club. Duncan's voice was urgent.

"Get back to the apartment as fast as you can make it. She's run out on us."

They were waiting for him, every light in the apartment burning. He came into the living-room slowly. Chalice and his partner were sitting side by side on the sofa. Neither man spoke as he went to the desk. The film and the prints were still in the drawer. He turned round slowly, knowing that the answer was expected of him. He hunched his shoulders.

"I don't know. I told you how I left her. She was going to stay here and not move. Where could she go—she didn't have a nickel." Still neither man spoke.

"If you're thinking of the police," he said suddenly "I don't believe it."

Chalice went to the mantelpiece. He picked up the bottle of sixpences, his mouth and eyes serious.

"This is Kathy's piggybank. She don't trust nobody. Look!" He held the bottle to the light. The level of the coins was well below the faint pencil-mark on the label. He replaced the bottle, his voice sombre. "I told you she smelled of trouble. And I was dead right."

Crying Eddie leant his head back, screwing up his face

as he watched Chalice cross the room to the bookcase. The older man pulled out the red-covered book. He pointed at the empty space behind.

"And she's a nut as well. That thing was loaded."

He stopped Duncan's rush towards the bedroom the girl had occupied.

"You won't find her there, mate. That's one favour she's done us."

He shook his head, aiming a blow at the squawking parrot as he passed. It subsided, eyeing him malevolently.

"You want to *know* where she's gone?" He answered his own question, pantomiming a trigger being pulled. "Number two, Elleston Place, that's where. I'm dead lucky that gun can't be traced to me. By now, Chelsea'll be about as healthy as the Central Criminal Court. That bird's going to blow holes in everyone she finds in the house."

Duncan blinked, trying desperately to think of a plausible alternative.

"But I watched the place for nearly three hours. She never came near. *Nobody* came near."

Crying Eddie moved easily, sitting upright. "How do *you* know? You say this geezer on the phone told her four o'clock. But she could have gone there earlier—long before you did, mate."

Duncan's control snapped. This was something tangible to deal with. He took three steps to the sofa and looked down at the other, his voice shaking.

"You're going to shout at me just too often—*mate*! Don't do it."

Crying Eddie answered mildly. "O k, o k. Still and all, what makes you so sure?"

The question drove holes through Duncan's certainty. He turned to Chalice.

"Look, Harry—I'm going back there—by myself. I want you two to stay here. The locks on the door are simple. All I need is a set of keys and a piece of loid—can you get those for me?"

Chalice's eyes transferred the question to his partner. Crying Eddie got up slowly.

"I'll be back in half-an-hour. Somebody ought to be thinking about a good mouthpiece. If you ask me, it's just about the right time for one."

Duncan wheeled the motor-cycle to the top of Elleston Place. He hid it out of sight in the passage at the back of the school playground. He walked slowly down towards the Embankment. The sky was high with bold stars nailed to it. A cold wind blew from the east, carrying the promise of snow. The street doors slammed behind him, marking the end of homebound journeys. Lights came on in hallways as he passed. A woman's voice called greetings—a child laughed.

The house with the green-painted door was still in complete darkness. He went up the steps casually, as if he had every right to be there. He turned with his back to the door. The pub across the street had opened for business but as yet there were no customers. He could see the girl behind the bar through the window—she was alone, knitting. He was screened by the porch from anyone not standing immediately in front of him. He shoved the pamphlets through, heard them drop and bent his head to the mailbox. Ears and nose told him nothing.

Two Elleston Place was listed in the Post Office Directory under the name of one Casimer Reidemister. He'd called the number from a booth. The ringing tone indicated a line out of order.

There were two locks on the front door, set close to one another at the height of his waist. He shone the pencil flash on the bottom lock. The bright, scratched metal casing showed that it had been used recently. He selected a key from the bunch Crying Eddie had delivered. The slender shaft had no stop-ring. The wards were fashioned in the basic pattern of a dropped E. He tried the key in the lock. The wards were too thick. His third choice slid home. He turned the shank, trying to lift the tumblers. He managed to raise them to a position of twelve o'clock—more than that they would not move. He held his left forefinger under the key, giving the wards the extra lift they needed The key engaged fully. His wrist described a circle and the lock was undone.

He pushed hard on the top of the right-hand door panel, sliding the six-inch strip of celluloid into the crack he had made between door and jamb. He brought the strip down till it hit the metal cup that held the spring-loaded tongue. A touch edged the end of the resilient material against the curved tongue. He increased the pressure, moving the door laterally. The celluloid strip bent, straightened, preventing the tongue from returning to its box. The weight of his shoulder pushed the door inwards and open. He shut it again quickly and stood motionless in the darkness.

An odd smell pervaded the hall, provoking a memory not quite complete. He moved forwards cautiously behind the narrow beam of the flashlight. Rolled carpets, tied round the middle, were upended against shrouded furniture. The acrid smell grew stronger as he neared a door on his right. As he turned the handle, he identified the stink of exploded cordite. The flash probed the room, touching a pile of ashes in the grate, a ransacked desk, an overturned standard lamp. He raised the beam slowly, searching the walls. A jagged hole scarred the ceiling high above the fireplace. Hope grew and then dwindled. Even if he could find the spent bullet it would mean nothing. There were seven other shells in the clip to be accounted for.

He looked down at the bare boards. A wide swathe had been cut in the dust from sofa to door 'as if a body had been dragged'. He ran upstairs, searching one room after another. Only one bedroom was furnished on the second storey. The bed had been slept in, the blankets and sheets left in an untidy jumble. Underclothes trailed from half-open drawers. A bowler hat was perched on a pair of folded trousers. Somebody in the next house pulled a plug in the bathroom. He shied from the sudden noise, moving away on the balls of his feet. He had reached the bottom of the stairs when he heard the sound of a car outside. He switched off his light and peered through the mailflap. A car was rolling down the ramp. The driver climbed out, standing for a moment in the full glare of his own head-lamps. He was thick-set, wearing a tweed hat and raglan coat. He bent down, hooking his hands in the iron grips and hoisting the cantilever door. When he turned into the light again, his face shone with sweat.

Duncan wasted no more time. The street door was only held on the Yale. He had to put the mortise lock on again. He dragged the keys from his pocket and worked frantic-ally. He succeeded in turning the key as the garage door rumbled down. He pulled the blackjack from his pocket, wrapping the cord firmly round his wrist. The leather sleeve was filled with buckshot. He heard the man coming up the steps walking like a man who carries too much weight. The visitor took his time with his keys, grunting as he stood in the open doorway, looking back up the street in both directions. As he stepped into the hall, Duncan swung his sap savagely. The blackjack thudded against the base of the man's neck, its end wrapping round his throat. He raised both hands like a diver going off the high board then pitched forward after his hat. Duncan hit him again in mid-air, a sharp blow high above the right ear. The man slumped, rolled over and lay perfectly still. Duncan peered from the threshold. The first customers were drinking in the pub. The sound of the swelling organ drifted down the quiet street. He shut the door firmly and bolted it top and bottom.

He crouched by the huddled body, the blackjack still swinging in his fingers. The man on the floor was breath-ing heavily, groaning at the finish of each exhalation. Dun-can took him by the ankles and shuffled backwards, pull-ing the man into the kitchen. Here uncurtained windows overlooked the roof of the garage. Enough light reflected from the street to allow him to see what he was doing. He dragged the unresisting form into the centre of the room and dropped the feet. They thudded heavily to the ground.

Ashe lay on his back, slack-jawed and snoring. His rucked-up trousers displayed a length of winter underwear. Duncan ran his hands through the other's pockets, tapping the mounds of flesh for a hidden weapon. He filled a jug at the sink and tipped it over the man's head. Ashe reacted immediately, turning his mouth away from the cascade of water that was drowning him. His hand crept a few inches. Duncan set his heel firmly on the man's wrist.

"Just one move out of place and I'll kill you—where's the girl?"

He bore down with his weight, hearing the watch-crystal crunch against the floorboards. The man's thick eyelids fluttered. The fingers of his free hand unclenched as if to hold Duncan's foot. The Canadian swung the sap, clouting Ashe's knuckles.

"The girl," he said again.

Spit bubbled in the corners of Ashe's mouth. He rolled his eyes towards the dripping faucet and groaned.

"Water!"

Duncan retreated to the sink warily. He refilled the jug and flung the contents into Ashe's face. The man gasped and half-struggled into a sitting position.

"Water!" said Duncan unsteadily. The church bell had started to toll monotonously, summoning worshippers through the cold to Evensong. The memory was remote and belonged to another world. Reality was a fat drenched killer watching for the first opening. Duncan turned one of the taps on the cooker. Gas hissed. He turned it off again and opened the oven door. Hatred hardened his voice.

"You set this thing up—you know the score. Your phone's cut off. There are no friends or neighbours worrying whether you're in bed with a bellyache. Just you and me. And nobody knows I'm here. It's cosy because I'm going to leave you with your head in the gas oven. It's a better deal than you've been offering around but just as final."

Ashe still sat up, supporting his weight on his hands. Blood trickled from his cut wrist. He looked from it to

Duncan, his wet face glistening. He seemed to have difficulty in speaking.

"Don't be a fool.. The very people you're protecting are you're enemies—not me. You're pushing yourself beyond your limits, Duncan. Don't fall into the trap and do their work."

Duncan switched on the flash and shone it full into Ashe's eyes. They were wide-open, grey and implacable. Duncan had the feeling the man would say more and that all of it would be lies. He steeled himself to bludgeon the truth from the reluctant mouth. He tossed the last chance at the other man.

"I want to know what you've done with the girl—that's for me—the rest can wait. You can't cop out any more, friend. You were right about my limits but I don't care. Whichever way this goes you're out of business. The road's finished for you right here in this room. If you won't talk to me you'll talk to the cops."

Ashe shook his head, mumbling as he bent, unfastening the watch-strap on his bloodstained wrist. He ducked suddenly, mouthing at the back of the watch before Duncan could stop him. His teeth crunched on something hidden. The poison acted immediately. His legs swept backwards so that he was kneeling. He started to drag himself painfully towards Duncan, eyes shut and arms flung out. He froze suddenly, jerked and toppled onto his face.

The faucet continued to drip noisily into the sink. Duncan silenced it mechanically. He looked down at Ashe's body. A strong smell of crushed almonds rose from the floor. He forced himself to go through the man's pockets again. There were no identifying papers. The labels sewn into the suit and overcoat were those of a chain-store tailor. The tweed hat might have been bought anywhere. He lifted Ashe's limp hand, feeling for a non-existent pulse. The emptiness of the house was suddenly frightening. He hurried into the hall, closing the street door after him with exaggerated care. The garage was unlocked. He recognized the M.G. as the car they had tried to kill him with. There were no documents in the glove compartment. He jotted down the number of the licence-tag. As he eased himself out of the driving-seat, his foot caught the edge of the rubber floormat. He bent down and picked up a flattened ball of paper. He smoothed out the creases. It was a magazine-wrapper bearing a stencilled address.

Roger Frew, M.D.
Hollow Oak
Dulwich Hill
S.E.

He rammed the scrap deep in the pocket of his overalls and dropped the cantilever door. The church bell was still tolling as he climbed the ramp to the street. He travelled back fast, filtering through the heavier traffic and dismounting wherever it helped. He left the machine in the bushes at the back of Chalice's apartment building and rode a service-elevator up to the penthouse. The kitchen door was unlocked. He walked through into the living-room. Chalice was lying on the sofa, legs crossed and his eyes shut. He opened them briefly as Duncan came in. Crying Eddie was leaning against the mantelpiece, attending to his nails. Duncan threw the helmet and goggles at a chair. He said nothing till he had poured himself a scotch. He lifted his glass at each man in turn.

"I guess you were right about the lawyer, Crying. I'm going to need one. I just left a dead man."

Chalice woke up. He box-shuffled a deck of cards as though his hands needed the exercise.

"That's handy," he said shortly.

Crying Eddie was picking at a torn cuticle on his thumb.

"What did you use on him?" he asked curiously.

The clock on the mantelpiece showed a few minutes to ten. The last hours seemed to have telescoped. Duncan's voice was a little shaky.

"Cyanide. I always carry some around with me."

Chalice looked at him sharply and put the deck of cards away.

"Let's stop the giggles—what happened, Ritchie?"

Duncan explained. ". . . someone had put a shot into the ceiling. But the girl wasn't there and the guy didn't talk."

The other two men looked at one another. Chalice nodded. Crying Eddie pulled a newspaper from his overcoat pocket. He folded it across the back page and gave it to Duncan.

"The stop press column."

The print was blurred, the brief report tucked away between the first results from the greyhound tracks.

Headless torso discovered on railway line near Lewisham. Body identified as Linda Swann, aged 27. Dead girl was under treatment for mental disorder and had absconded from asylum near Ascot. Police spokesman rules out possibility of foul play.

He tore the newspaper across the middle and pitched the pieces into the fireplace. He stood for a while, staring through the open door at the bed where she had slept. More than anything it was her loneliness that he remembered. She'd been weak, foolish and sentimental—and desperately lonely. He spoke with angry determination.

"I know what you're both thinking—that you ought to be beating my head in. It's too late for that now. There *is* only one way out—we've got to go to the police."

Crying Eddie put his nail-file away, his young face morose. "Fine thing. All my life without getting my collar felt now I got to walk in with a couple of jail-birds and explain what I'm doing lumbered-up with dead bodies. Come to that —I wish somebody would *tell* me what I'm doing with 'em!"

Chalice scowled, raising a clenched fist threateningly. "Why don't you shut up with your 'dead bodies'! We ain't *done* nothing, for Gawd's sake! Ritchie's right—what do you want to do—sit here and wait for them to fetch us. We got to be first."

Crying Eddie laughed shortly. "Whichever way it is, they're going to be real friendly. I can just see 'em when you get round to explaining why that bird was brought here in the first place. We'll be eating porridge for the next five years, if you ask me."

Duncan pushed between them. "Nobody *is* asking you. We're going to call the Yard first and then take the film to them."

Crying Eddie reknotted his tie in front of the mirror. "Nice," he said bitterly. "My old lady's going to love all this. All our relations round home pulling up the floorboards looking for my money. I want my brains testing ever listening to you two."

Chalice shifted to the phone. He picked up the receiver gingerly, then replaced it.

"You got a better speaking voice than I have, Crying. It don't sound right coming from me."

"Don't sound *what*?" Crying Eddie said incredulously. His face grew dangerously red. "A better speaking voice! You must be joking. What's the matter with 'im—he knows more about it than I do." He jerked a thumb at Duncan.

The Canadian opened a drawer in the desk. He sat by the phone with the film and prints on the table in front of him. He shrugged and then dialled. A voice answered the first ring.

"New Scotland Yard—Information Room—can I help you?"

Duncan cleared his throat. "I want to report a murder, officer."

"May I have your name, please?"

"Didn't you hear what I said," Duncan replied clearly. "A murder. Put me on to somebody in authority."

He held the receiver away from his ear. A second voice followed a series of crackles—a deep voice with a North Country accent.

"Detective-Superintendent Vogal speaking."

Chalice and Crying Eddie moved closer to the phone, straining their ears to listen. Duncan pulled the magazine-wrapper from his pocket and smoothed the creases on his knee.

"My name's Ritchie Duncan. I'm speaking for three of us

—we'll be with you in half-an-hour's time. This is urgent. A girl was killed tonight—the story's in the Late Night Extra edition of the Standard. I'm sure she was murdered. I'm going to give you the name and address of the man you want to interrogate and you'd better be quick. Roger Frew, Hollow Oak, Dulwich Hill."

The cop's voice was incisive. "I have that, yes. Where are you speaking from?"

"Primrose 0009," Duncan answered. "This isn't a hoax. I've got a film in my hand and some prints. The film was stolen from Faraday Electronic Research at Hampton Court. I believe that three people have died as a direct result. I'm going to read the heading across the top of one of the prints. 'Project A. Lederle, TOP SECRET.' There's one last thing before I come in, Superintendent—you'd better check my name with the Criminal Records Office. I'll give it you again —Ritchie Duncan. R-i-t-c-h-i-e."

He hung up. Each man looked at the phone as if he expected it to break into a violent and immediate ringing. Duncan broke the spell.

"I'll get dressed. You'd better get rid of those keys and stuff, Harry. Leave this place clean. They'll be up here later."

He heard them moving about as he changed into his grey flannel suit. There were papers burning in the grate when he went back to the living-room. Chalice had made a pile of the equipment. He wrapped the keys, celluloid and black-jack in a piece of newspaper. Duncan followed him out to the kitchen. Chalice opened the back door and brought the service elevator to the top. He bent down, poking the package under the bottom of the cage. It fell to the bottom of the shaft. He wiped and dried his hands at the kitchen sink.

"O k, mates," he said heavily. "Let's get it over with."

They were walking across the forecourt to the parked Jaguar when the squad cars turned in from the street. There were four of them, each with its two outriders. The speed-cops fanned left and right cutting off escape on all sides. Exhausts stuttered throatily. The three men stood blinking, ringed by headlights. Plain clothes men piled from the squad cars. Duncan shaded his eyes from the glare. Somebody grabbed him by the elbow and hustled him into the nearest squad car. The door slammed. The man sitting next to the driver bent into a microphone. Duncan looked back. The other two were being pulled into one of the vehicles behind. The front of the apartment-building was dotted with hastily-opened windows. Tenants and porters thronged the entrance-lobby excitedly, watching as the cortège roared up the quiet road.

The radio-operator's voice vied with the whine of the powerful motor, issuing a steady stream of instructions. Duncan shook his arm free angrily.

"Get your goddam hands off me! What in hell is this anyway?"

The man on his right wore no hat and drab, shapeless clothes. He swivelled his head towards Duncan, his long neck poking from a high starched collar.

"Take it easy, lad," he said quietly.

Duncan repeated the words indignantly. "Take it easy?" Then he moved his shoulders philosophically. "O k—if it's going to be like that. Am I allowed to smoke or is it going to be one of those tough sessions?"

The cop on his left struck a match and held the flame to Duncan's cigarette.

"Do as Superintendent Vogal told you—take it easy."

Duncan smoked in silence. The cortège raced south, sticking to the crown of the highway. The motorcycle escort travelled ahead, holding the traffic at intersections even when the signals were in its favour. Big Ben was chiming the half-hour as they swung into the yard behind Whitehall. They used the back way into the tall dour building. Vogal's office was reached through a warren of passages. The noise of their arrival opened doors where lights were still burning. These doors closed hurriedly as the occupants of the rooms recognized Vogal's spare head. Chalice and his partner stayed close to Duncan. A uniformed officer ushered them into a small office. Through the wide-open windows, the lights of Westminster Bridge spanned the river. The noise of the Embankment traffic was a grumble far below.

The furniture and lighting were primitive. The Detective-Superintendent dismissed everyone but the man who had been with him in the car. He sat behind a plain deal table and indicated his aide.

"This is Detective-Sergeant Rosskelly." He stared down at the papers in front of him. "Duncan, Chalice and Ward. An odd combination. Which of you has the film?"

Duncan laid the small package on the table. Vogal handed it to his subordinate who hurried from the room with it. Voices were raised along the passage. A door slammed. Vogal frowned.

"There's one thing I want each one of you to understand from the start. As far as I am concerned you all came here voluntarily. What police action was taken was taken for your own protection. Is that quite clear?"

Crying Eddie fixed his eyes on a small microphone on the table. He smiled as if he had just bitten on something unexpected at a friend's dinner-party.

"Can I go home, then. My mother will be worried."

Vogal had the drawn face of an insomniac. It was obvious that his patience was thin.

"I said that you came here voluntarily. If you don't like the idea I can always find something to hold you on. Would you prefer that?"

Chalice trod hard on Crying Eddie's foot. He disassociated himself from Duncan loftily.

"You've got us all wrong, Uncle Bill. We're only keeping him company."

The Canadian agreed. "That's right enough, Superintendent. I'm the guy with the answers."

Crying Eddie pushed his hands deeper into his overcoat pockets. His expression was tolerant.

"You see, Uncle Bill, you're making a big mistake. I told you—my old mum'll be worried."

Vogal's eyes were the colour of old slate. The calmness of his voice added to its menace.

"The next one of you to call me 'Uncle Bill' is going to regret it. An E-type Jaguar was used in Ascot last night—a girl was abducted from a mental home. The number of the car is EPB 500. You, Ward, drove it and you, Chalice, own it. Now get outside, the pair of you and do a little hard thinking. Duncan, you stay."

Rosskelly opened the door. As soon as they were alone, Vogal's manner changed completely. He looked like a man faced with a difficult problem. His voice hardened with his intensity, tapping on the base of the microphone with a discoloured fingernail.

"Every word said in this room will be heard by other people as soon as I switch this thing on. I'm told there's a good reason for it. I know a little about you, Duncan. That's why I'm telling you this privately—you *were* in danger. You've been in danger ever since you left Elleston Place tonight."

Duncan swallowed hard, seeing the dim kitchen, the prostrate body, its knees drawn to its belly in dying agony. He made no answer.

The pencil went round and round in Vogal's fingers. He leant across the table.

"We're on the same side, lad, whether you like it or not."

Duncan answered unsteadily. "The hell we are. What is this—one of these big deals you guys cook up—with handshakes all round at the end of it all and somebody's name in the Honours List? I'm blasé, Superintendent—I'm not impressed by the mystique and the production. Where you are I don't know but for once *I'm* on the right side. A girl's been murdered—do you understand that—*murdered*."

The pencil snapped in Vogal's fingers. "I'm an officer of the Metropolitan Police Force—that means something to me. I'm also sufficiently old-fashioned to be able to obey orders without question. Your answers will have to come from someone else. Time's getting short. Do you want to tell your story or not?"

Big Ben chimed the quarter. No more than fifteen minutes had passed since they had brought him here yet it seemed an eternity. Duncan nodded slowly.

"That's why I came."

Vogal threw the switch on the microphone. His tired face took on an official expression.

"You are Ritchie Duncan, Canadian, thirty-seven years of age. You are making this statement of your own free will. I want you to start from the day you left prison."

Duncan dragged his chair nearer the microphone. He spoke carefully and without useless repetition, editing only the frustration and bitterness of the last few days. He ended the statement defiantly.

"I still know the meaning of an oath—I swear this to be the truth, so help me God!"

He looked away, disturbed by the ring of melodrama in the words. Vogal turned off the machine, his eyes kindly.

"You know, son, I meant it when I said we were on the same side. Try to remember that no matter what you think is going on."

Duncan pushed back his chair. "This is only the beginning, isn't it, Superintendent?'

Vogal was silent for a moment. "Only the beginning," he said reluctantly. "They're going to take you somewhere else. It'll be a while before the people come for you. You'd better have a bite down in the canteen while you're waiting."

Duncan went to the door. He felt a cop's hand on his shoulder without threat for the first time. He turned the handle. Chalice and his partner were waiting along the passage, eyeing their escort nervously. Vogal beckoned one of the detectives.

"Take these men to the canteen, I'll ring down when I want them."

The large cafeteria smelled of stewing tea and bacon sandwiches. Groups of police were either standing around or sitting, in and out of uniform. A few looked up with interest as the five men came into the canteen. They carried their cups to a table, their escort staying just out of earshot. Crying Eddie's jaws worked incessantly as he stared down the curious eyes about him. He sipped the dark brown liquid in his cup, spat and wiped his lips fastidiously.

"I'm going to ask these charlies what they're looking at in a minute," he said to the other two.

Chalice hid his face in his hands as a tall plain-clothesman detached himself from a group nearby. The cop was dressed in square-toed shoes and an Italian-style suit. He stank of beer and his eyes were a little too bright. He looked from Chalice to Ward, affecting startled surprise. Then he bit into his sandwich, addressing the room in general through a mouthful of food.

"How about that—the terrible twins! Poor sods—what you doing mixed up with the murder-squad, fellers?"

"Beat it," Duncan said in a low distinct voice. He didn't want to look at either of the others.

The man grinned. "They say it's painless—if your neck breaks. I'll see what I can do for Kathy—she's going to be lonely."

Duncan caught Chalice halfway out of his seat and pulled him down again. One of the escorts moved to the table, grimfaced. He put himself squarely in front of the young officer.

"Where are you stationed?"

The youngster steadied himself to a semblance of attention.

"L Division, sir."

The escort's voice was curt. "Then get back there."

The canteen was hushed as the man left, then a babble broke out louder than the clatter of crockery. Crying Eddie looked across the table at his partner.

"Uncle Bill's the murder squad? What's he talking about, Harry?"

Chalice's eyes roved the room nervously. He answered in distrait fashion.

"Ah, forget it. He's one of them flash coppers out of Islington, isn't he? He was kidding." He was quiet for a moment. "Wasn't he, Ritchie?"

Duncan's stomach was uneasy. "He wasn't kidding, no,

Harry. Vogal says they're taking us somewhere else—I don't know what for or where. But you're both in the clear—I can swear to that." He rose to his feet as the two detectives walked towards them.

They travelled in a staid topheavy limousine driven by a uniformed chauffeur with sidewhiskers. The three men sat on the back seat facing Vogal and Rosskelly. The Superintendent was wearing a flat-brimmed bowler-hat set squarely on his head. They turned north out of Victoria Street into one of the squares that are normally deserted by 5 p.m. The Queen Anne house had long-since been converted to offices for yacht-brokers and civil engineers. The car stopped in front of white-painted railings where an unobtrusive sign read:

Forbes, Sperry and Losch.

There was no further indication of the firm's function. A couple of television cameras set in the wall were trained on the street door. This was opened by someone inside as the group of men came from the car. The rectangular hall was panelled in light walnut. An eighteenth-century chest did service as coat-rack. There were candles in silver holders— a telephone housed in a sedan-chair. The offbeat note was the sound of a teletype machine chattering up in the darkened second storey. A youngish man came down the stairs, taking them two at a time. He greeted Vogal familiarly and looked at the three men.

"Which one's mine, Superintendent?"

Chalice and his partner were suddenly interested in their shoes. Vogal touched Duncan's arm. The man smiled mechanically.

"Will you come this way, Mr. Duncan?"

He tapped on a door across the hall, opened and closed it leaving Duncan inside. The room was furnished with a great deal of leather. There were no prints or paintings, the only decoration a china horse rearing on the mantelpiece. A couple of well-sprung chairs had been dragged in front of the leaping fire. A large blond man had forced his frame into one of them. He was untidily dressed in shaggy grey checks and wore tinted spectacles with curved lenses. He spoke in a voice that was low-pitched yet authoritative—as if he were accustomed to giving orders that were never questioned.

"Please sit down."

Duncan lowered himself cautiously. The staging was effective. First the bleak corridors of the Yard with the hint of a cell and handcuffs, then this quiet warm room where even the tick of the clock seemed to hold mannered welcome.

"You're an intelligent chap," the blond man said quietly. "You probably have your own ideas about who I am and why you have been brought here?"

Duncan gave it a moment's thought. "I don't think I'd recognize a good idea if you put a collar and leash on it. I have a strong feeling that you represent trouble—that's about as far as I go."

The man turned his hands over. For someone of his size they were oddly fleshless and sensitive.

"Then I'd better put your mind at rest. My name is Hamilton. I'm certainly not a policeman in the sense that you know them. I don't even enforce the law. My sole interest in you stems from an entirely selfish reason, Mr Duncan. Out of fifty million people in the country you're the only one who can help me. My problem is that I don't know whether you *will*. Please smoke. You'll find cigarettes in the box on the table beside you. Virginia on the left, Turkish on the right." His face tilted at a strange angle.

Duncan was suddenly aware that Hamilton was blind. The eyes behind the tinted lenses were looking over the Canadian's shoulder. The silver box had a depression in the lid. Duncan guessed that an inscription had at some time been erased. The teletype machine broke into a clatter again as he lit a cigarette.

"What am I supposed to say to that, Mr Hamilton? I don't even begin to know what you're talking about. You say I can help you. If it's true give me one good reason why I should."

Hamilton dragged up a sock, his fingers lingering to scratch his ankle.

"I'll have to answer that obliquely. I'm afraid that nothing I could have done would have saved Linda Swann. We were three hours too late for that. In fact, I've been too late ever since Seiler arrived in the country. I might not have been had you decided to go to the police earlier."

A pattern was shaping slowly in Duncan's mind but the name Seiler found no place in it.

"Seiler?" he repeated.

Hamilton's hands juggled an invisible ball. "Anton Seiler —Dr. Roquemaure—Henry Ashe. He had many names. He could have told us a great deal, Mr Duncan. But these chaps are disciplined and a cyanide pill is standard equipment. Of course you had no way of knowing this."

Hamilton's spectacles reflected the firelight. His face was bland and courteous. Duncan lifted his head. In three minutes he had been saddled with the responsibility for two deaths. The implication was that he had no choice but to do as Hamilton wanted. He flicked an inch of ash into the fireplace.

"You're right. I had no way of knowing anything. Nor had Linda Swann. Nobody told us. Who was *Ashe*—some sort of agent?"

The blind man's expression was thoughtful. "The description does him an injustice. He was a scholar, an assassin, a man of deep convictions, an authority on the use of psychotomimetics. He was all these. His death was desirable but untimely."

The quiet contemplative voice, the precise language, angered Duncan. Bitterness and frustration forced themselves into his answer.

"I know blindness is supposed to be sacrosanct but I'm going to give this to you straight, Mr Hamilton. What right do you have to involve innocent people in your shenanigans? I can only guess what the film represents and Ashe's connection with it. Can't you understand that I don't *give* a goddam about it—that I'm in this simply because I lost a

job and two people tried to kill me? I'm not in it for glory—
that's your department. What kind of guy are you anyway,
sitting behind dark glasses, smiling while people have died?"

Hamilton's head tilted as he listened intently to the sound
of Duncan's heavy breathing. He answered patiently.

"As long as the issues are clear between us, our opinion
of one another doesn't really matter. I wouldn't be here if I
had to justify my actions. I'm afraid you credit me with
more knowledge and ability than I really have. We knew
nothing about this film until you told us. All we knew was
that Ashe was in England. That in itself warranted appre-
hension. Your statement to the police has been invaluable.
Please help me put it into practice."

Duncan set his mouth obstinately. "Since when are your
problems mine? You people make me sick—you're so goddam smug. You kick a man in the balls and then expect him
to believe in pacifism."

Hamilton lifted himself from his chair and felt his way
across the room to a drawer. He came back carrying a small
cardboard box. He sat down, opened the box and showed
Duncan the spent rifle bullet nestling in the bed of cotton.
He weighed it in his hand for a moment, then took off his
spectacles. The thick tortoiseshell frames concealed a small
scar above each temple. He put his spectacles on again.

"Vienna 1952—from the roof of a house occupied by the
same Henry Ashe. Only he was Anton Seiler in those days
and a Stalinist. You're an intelligent man. I refuse to believe
that you're indifferent to the dangers that confront western
civilization. I'll go further than that—I think you're the sort
of man who'll want to oppose them—if only because a girl
has been wantonly killed."

Duncan's answer was what he had known it would be
from the start.

"You don't have to run the flag up the pole—I'll salute
it down here. You can count me in, Mr. Hamilton. But for
none of the reasons you've given. It's an odd thing but I'll
be thumbing my nose at the whole bunch of you. You won't
understand and yet it's true."

175

"I understand all right," Hamilton said softly. "I understand perfectly. The man whose name you supplied—Frew —I want him alive, Mr. Duncan."

A sense of savage satisfaction surged in Duncan. He felt like a man who has been fighting in the dark and who sees his opponent clearly for the first time—rocking and ready for the kill.

"Where is he?" he asked.

Hamilton leaned back in his chair and locked his hands.

"On the *M.V. Dahomey*—a Costa-Rican registered freighter under charter to a firm in Antwerp. At the moment she's tied up at Rotherhithe unloading fifty tons of boxed dates. She's due to sail on the morning tide. Dr. Frew's occupying the captain's cabin. He appears on the ship's papers in the name of Martin Walpole. It's the name on the passport he's using as well." The details seemed to give him satisfaction. He nodded and smiled.

Duncan had a picture of a launch drifting through the darkness—of men clambering up the blind side of a moored freighter.

"What's the matter with the police?" he asked quietly.

"Impossible," said Hamilton. "I couldn't put a man aboard that boat without Frew realizing that the game was up. He'd be dead before they reached him. I can't afford to let that happen again."

Duncan said it without too much conviction. "Then where do I come in—as a lure to get him off the boat?"

"Exactly," nodded Hamilton. "There's no way in which he could know about Ashe's death. We removed the body from Elleston Place half-an-hour after you left. Frew no longer cares about the film. He knows that steps have been taken to render the information useless. The danger signal's up and they're all running. I want Frew to think that Ashe had tricked you into some form of alliance. Tricked— forced—cajoled—it doesn't matter as long as he believes it. Frew is intelligent, wary and ruthless—their best man next to Ashe. Get him off that boat and you'll have done more than my agency has been able to do."

"And how do I do it?"

Hamilton's smile had the peculiar sweetness of the blind. "Frew can see. I hope he lives to regret it. Will you please tell Superintendent Vogal I'd like to speak to him."

Duncan went out to the hall. The strangers guarding the door looked like junior masters at some good prep school. Crying Eddie was sitting on the bottom rung of the staircase. Chalice hung moodily over the banister watching Duncan's expression. The Canadian had no time to explain. Vogal strode from Hamilton's room a purposeful look on his face. He tapped Chalice on the shoulder.

"Hop it—and take that tailor's advertisement with you. The next time I run into either of you be prepared for trouble. Now get out!"

Crying Eddie came to his feet promptly. He picked a thread from his immaculate trousers. He grinned at Vogal.

"Gawd love yer, mate! One of the kindest men I ever knew. I'm dead sorry I called you Uncle Bill!"

Chalice looked at Duncan uncertainly. "What about our mate—ain't he coming with us?"

"You just lost him," answered Vogal. "If he's got any sense he'll make the arrangement permanent. Now get out of here before I pinch the pair of you for loitering with intent to commit a felony. Go on, get out of it!"

The two men walked towards the door. As it opened, Duncan lifted his hand in salute.

Duncan moved forward cautiously, shutting his nostrils against the ammoniac reek of the fouled walls. The alley was narrow, a short cut that led from the dockside to the busy highway running parallel to the waterfront. Stone pillars at each end of the alley barred the way to motorized traffic. The *M.V. Dahomey* loomed over the low warehouses flanking the dock gates. The boat was a thousand tonner with the lines of a deep-sea trader. Smoke trickled from a dirty-white funnel bearing three green stars. The floodlights from a mobile crane shed a harsh radiance over the bridge and the forrard half of the boat. The crane grab worked methodically, hoisting boxes slung in netting. A steady stream of bilge followed a rust-streaked course down the side of the vessel. A donkey-engine aft strained against a wire hawser.

Duncan lifted his gaze to the boat's riding-lights. They appeared to swing in wide arcs against the sky, despite the calm water. He looked over to the bridge. The angle of vision was oblique and offered no more than a narrowed glimpse of the interior. A man in a blue cap was lolling against the wheel, talking to someone out of sight. As Duncan heard the sound of the car, he checked his watch. The vehicle ghosted from the far end of the square and stopped in front of a service station that was closed for the night. Someone bleeped the horn three times, very softly.

Duncan stepped out of the alley. Warehouses and the dock-gates formed the northern side of the rough square, the entire space ablaze in the glare from the crane and the boat. The division of light and shade was sharp. Over on the south side of the square the only light in the shadows was a neon strip over a small café. Duncan hurried along the pavement, past closed ship-chandlers and insurance offices to the gas-station. He stood for a while, hidden by the pumps. The arm of the crane lifted high above the level of the low roofs then dipped out of sight. Chains rattled and a man shouted.

Duncan bent low and ran round to the offside of the parked car. He opened the door and took his place behind the wheel. The motor was running. He looked up into the driving-mirror and turned away quickly. Ashe's body was wedged upright in a corner of the back seat, his arms stiff by his side. The tweed hat was set rakishly on his head. His eyes had been opened, his clothes rearranged. His mouth hung slightly open as though he were about to say something. The man crouching on the floor at his feet spoke quietly.

"Move the car into the light. As you get out, turn round as if you're talking to him. I'll do the rest."

Duncan engaged the gears. He drove as far as the railings at the end of the warehouse and killed the motor. A hundred yards away, the bows of the *Dahomey* lifted on the faint swell. From this angle Duncan had a full view of the bridge. The blue-capped man was alone now, his back to the car. His shadow grew long as he bent in front of the instrument panel. Duncan heard a bell ring. The donkey-engine stopped. He turned in his seat, repeating his instructions for the last time.

"I walk from the boat to the café. I stand in the window. When I'm ready I signal."

"With your *left* hand," the voice insisted. "We'll only have one crack at him—no more. Just do your best."

The body on the rear seat moved slightly as the speaker manipulated it into some semblance of life. Duncan hurried towards the dock-gates. The wooden hut on the right was empty. He lifted the bar and walked onto the pier. The warehouse doors were open, revealing a vault-like expanse of cold-storage units. The *Dahomey* bumped steadily against her fenders, her mooring chains clinking. A dozen yards away, the crane straddled its railway lines on spindly legs. A man with an eyeshade was supervising the loading of an electric dumper. The gangway climbed up steeply to the deck, thirty feet over Duncan's head. He shouted up.

"Is anyone there?"

One of the curtained portholes was lighted, the rest were dim circles in the black hull. He walked a few yards up the gangway, shielding his eyes and calling again.

"Ahoy there!"

A slight movement from behind a ventilator caught his eye. A man crossed the deck and stood for a second staring over the side at Duncan. Then he disappeared behind a lifeboat. Duncan swung round as he heard the angry shouting behind him. A dock policeman came running from the warehouse, redfaced with indignation.

"What the hell do you think you're doing. You just can't walk in here like that—where's your pass?"

Duncan was certain that he was still being watched from the deck above. He made his voice apologetic.

"I'm sorry, officer—I didn't know. I wanted to see someone aboard this ship. It's all right—I'll go."

The cop used his belly as a buffer, pushing Duncan towards the gates.

"That's all well and good. This is a customs area— you don't go walking on and off boats without the proper authority."

He slammed the bar down and stood at the gates watching Duncan walk to the neon sign on the far side of the square. The shadows had changed form and substance subtly. As Duncan passed the alley he was aware of the men standing there, flattened against the walls. A furniture-removal truck was parked in the forecourt of the gas-station, lights out and apparently empty. He pushed the door of the café. There was no one there but the man behind the counter. His hairy chest and arms thrust from a soiled singlet. He looked up from his sheaf of football coupons, licking the stub of pencil. He held a mug under the spigot of a hissing tea-urn, wheeled and set it in front of Duncan. His accent belied his scruffiness.

"They've cleared the line. You give this number and ask for the boat."

He shrugged as though asked a question and pointed at the telephone indifferently. He lowered the volume on the tinny radio behind him and went back to his football coupons. Duncan took the phone. The length of flex allowed him to carry the receiver to the window. The glass and chrome of the parked car winked in the light. The body in the back had been slightly shifted. It now bent forward slightly as if with expectancy. The square waited in silence. The rhythm aboard the *Dahomey* was unchanged. Duncan picked up the receiver from its rest.

"Tower 0770—shore-to-ship service. I want to talk to the *M.V. Dahomey*—she's lying at pier 1, Rotherhithe Docks." The operator connected him immediately.

The reply came, heavily accented. *"Ja, M.V. Dahomey* here."

Duncan's left shoulder was to the window. "I want to talk to Mr. Walpole—it's urgent and personal."

There was a pause, a scraping sound, then the monosyllable, flat and unencouraging.

"Yes?"

Duncan lowered his voice. "Mr. Walpole?"

"Who are you and what do you want?" demanded the other.

Duncan spaced his words to give them emphasis. "I'm Ritchie Duncan—I think you know the name. I'm phoning from a café immediately across the square—you can see it from the boat. I have a message for you from a friend. An *urgent* message."

He looked across at the boat as the silence stretched. Two men were silhouetted against the port windows of the bridge. The blue-capped officer and the watcher from the deck. He kept his eyes on the bridge, his neck now sweating. Frew turned his shoulders very slowly as if drawn by a magnet. Then he came to the window. The two men stared at one another across the square.

Frew's tone was sharp but perfectly controlled. "What is the message?"

Duncan talked rapidly. "There's a gas-station on the corner—some railings in front of it. You should be able to see the car that's parked there. He's sitting in the back seat with a bullet in his leg. I've brought him as far as I can —it's up to you now."

The man behind the counter folded his coupons and moved quietly into a back room. A ship's siren haunted the lower reaches of the river. A dog trotted along the sidewalk outside, sniffed the air and then scuttled into the shadows. The movement on the bridge was quick and decisive. As Frew levelled a pair of night-glasses on the parked car, Duncan laid his left hand flat upon the window-pane. The body in the back of the car stirred. An arm lifted slowly as if with pain and effort and then the body slumped sideways.

The sound of scraping feet filled the earpiece, Frew's voice was harsh and disturbed.

"Meet me at the dock-gates, I'm coming ashore."

Duncan cradled the phone. He replaced it on the counter seeing the shake in his fingers and not caring. The man in the singlet looked at him narrowly.

"Watch his hands—don't worry about anything else—just watch his hands. And wait for the lights."

Duncan opened the door and started across tarmac glistening with mist off the river. Frew was coming down the gangway on the run. The tall bent figure halted briefly at the gates. Frew said something to the cop in the box. The man raised the barrier. Duncan quickened his step. They met a couple of hundred feet from the parked car. Frew was carrying a small case in his left hand, his right was hidden in his overcoat pocket.

"Is he hit above or below the knee?"

"The groin," said Duncan. "He's lost a lot of blood."

Frew started to run. Bright headlights suddenly stabbed the darkness. Duncan jumped on Frew's back as the removal truck lurched forward. He locked his hands over the doctor's mouth. Frew's nails scored the Canadian's skin. Duncan held on grimly, his palms blocking access to the other's lips. They wrestled to the ground, the burst instrument-case spilling bottles and bandages. Men clambered down from the truck, adding their weight to Duncan's. Someone swung a truncheon. He felt Frew's body go limp. Duncan crawled out of the tangle of arms and legs. He sat down heavily on the kerb, looking at the blood oozing from his raked skin.

Men were carrying Frew to a waiting car—others were running up the gangway to the *Dahomey*. A searchlight pierced the gathering mist in midstream. Whistles blew on a police launch. He put his head between his knees and vomited. When he looked up, Superintendent Vogal was watching him from the back of a squad car.

"You need your bed," Vogal said. "Come on, we'll give you a lift home, lad."

Duncan got up slowly. He wrapped a handkerchief round

his bloodied knuckles. He felt automatically for his passport, its outline in an inside pocket reassuring.

"Did you say 'home', Superintendent?" he asked unsteadily.

They looked at one another for a long, hard second, then the policeman shut the door again.

"Good luck," he said quietly.

Duncan smiled because anything else would have been pointless and started walking across the square.